amazing india

A State-by-State Guide

Written by
Anita Vachharajani

Illustrated and designed by
Amit Vachharajani

SCHOLASTIC
New York Toronto London Auckland Sydney
Mexico City New Delhi Hong Kong Buenos Aires

In memory of Sriram, who knew so much

Anita Vachharajani enjoys writing stories and books for children. She has a keen interest in places, people and art, and loves books of all shapes and sizes.

Amit Vachharajani juggles two loves—film-making and illustrating books. He is a compulsive doodler and a passionate collector of children's picture books.
Anita and Amit live in Mumbai with their daughter .

Maps by **Aditya Menon**

Many thanks to everyone who was with us on this journey of discovery: to Amma, who has helped us cheerfully in countless ways and at all times; to Nayana, without whose relentless questioning this book wouldn't have been as much fun; and to everyone who carefully sifted through the text—Tina Narang, Sachin Balwalli, Sudha Raghavendran, and especially Akhila Naik, for her careful and thorough reading.

Every effort has been made to get the latest and most accurate information about each Indian state. The author and publishers would be grateful if any inadvertent errors are brought to their notice.

Published by Scholastic India Pvt. Ltd.
A subsidiary of Scholastic Inc., New York, 10012 (USA).
Publishers since 1920, with international operations in Canada, Australia, New Zealand, the United Kingdom, Mexico, India, Argentina, and Hong Kong.

For information regarding permission, write to:
Scholastic India Pvt. Ltd.
Golf View Corporate Tower-A, 3rd Floor,
DLF Phase-V, Gurgaon-122002 (India)

First edition: June 2009

ISBN 10: 81-8477-280-7
ISBN 13: 978-81-8477-280-7

Printed at Rave India, New Delhi

Introduction

Shiver in the snowy desert of Ladakh, or sweat in the hot, sandy desert of the Rann of Kutchch. Walk among models of prehistoric animals in the fossil park of Saketi, or take a living root bridge across a river in Meghalaya. Watch butterfly fish flit in and out of atolls—the coral islands of Lakshadweep—or explore a haunted fort inside one of Rajasthan's tiger reserves. See the many ways in which prehistoric man left his mark in the ancient caves of Madhya Pradesh, Uttarakhand and Kerala; or walk through the snaking corridors of underground caves in Andhra Pradesh, where a rock formation looks like a banyan tree.

Come with us and explore the cultural, artistic, historic and geographic diversity of India, the seventh largest country of the world. India is dotted with mountain ranges, snowy deserts, sandy deserts, plains, marshes, coral islands, coasts and grasslands. Each of these geographical features has a unique ecosystem, with an astonishing variety of animals, birds, plants and flowers.

In *Amazing India,* you can meet a few of them. Read about the binturong of Northeast India which isn't a bear or a cat—but is sometimes called a 'bearcat'. Or the hoolock gibbon—the subcontinent's only ape—which swings from tree to tree and 'sings' to its mate! Lion-tailed macaques (no relations of the big cats), dancing deer, clouded leopards, dugongs, hornbills, sooty terns, kaleej pheasants, tragopans and pitcher plants—all await you inside these pages!

Naturally, India's geographical diversity is also reflected in its regional art forms as well. The birds, insects, animals, flowers, soil or trees found in each region influence its dances, arts and crafts. Clothes, music, food and religious practices also seem to magically change with the changing landscape.

Sadly, a lot of India's beauty and diversity are at risk today. Many languages and art forms are being forgotten slowly. People are being forced to give up ways of living which protected their forests and their land. Tigers, red pandas, giant squirrels, Olive Ridley turtles and binturongs are just a few of the many species that are dying out because their habitats are being destroyed.

In *Amazing India* we share and celebrate the joy of being a part of India's dazzling diversity. Come with us to take a peek into the lives of the different people who live here—along with the birds, plants and insects whose songs they have sung and drawn for centuries.

Here is *Amazing India*, yours to protect, preserve and treasure!

There are some words in this book that you may not have read before. When you see this sign ❓ go to page 69 and 70. You will find a detailed explanation there.

Contents

Abbreviations used:

NP	-	National Park
WS	-	Wildlife Sanctuary
BC	-	Before Christ
AD	-	Anno Domini
m	-	metre
ft	-	foot or feet
sq km	-	square kilometres

Jammu & Kashmir is a vast and spectacularly beautiful region. It is, however, marked by various border disputes. A 'Line of Control' defined in 1972 divides it into Indian- and Pakistani-administered parts. China controls parts of the Aksai Chin region of Ladakh. These divisions are not recognised by the Indian government.

The name Kashmir probably comes from two words—'ka' meaning water, and 'shmir' meaning desiccated or dried. According to legend, it was created when Sage Kashyapa drained a lake. Locals call it Kashir.

Buddhist, Hindu and Sufi-Islamic philosophies mingled here to form a **blend of religions** which brought people together. In the isolated Kargil region of Ladakh, many Buddhist and Islamic practices have merged.

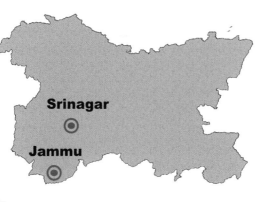

Srinagar

Jammu

Kashmir was an important centre of Hinduism, and later, of Buddhism, which was brought here by Ashoka in 300 BC. He also founded the ancient city of Srinagar. In 1349, Shah Mirza founded the Salatin-i-Kashmir dynasty. The Sikhs took over in 1819, followed by the Dogras who ruled under the British from 1846.

Ranging from 5500 to 14,000 ft, the 141-sq-km **Dachigam NP** lies in the Zabarwan range. It is enclosed by two steep ridges, has upper and lower sectors, and varied habitats. Migratory ducks, wild goats, ibexes, snow leopards, monal pheasants and hanguls live here.

Kashmir is marked by high mountains, deep valleys and lofty, inhospitable plateaus. It is separated from Jammu by the Himalayan foothills and the Pir Panjal range. The Kashmir Valley, 1600 m high, is very fertile. The **Ladakh** plateau lies to the northeast. It is made up of two districts: Leh and Kargil.

Kashmiri food is a blend of Buddhist, Pandit, Central Asian, Persian, Afghan and Punjabi cuisines. Traditionally, Kashmiri Pandits eat meat, but avoid onions and garlic. The **wazwan** or traditional feast of Kashmiri Muslims is spread over 36 courses. A team of chefs led by the Vasta Waza or head chef cooks the food.

The **hangul** or Kashmir stag is the only species of European red deer found in India. It has majestic antlers. In the 1940s, there were about 5000 left. Only 150 remained in 1970. With conservation, their numbers rose by 1980, but dropped again by 2008.

The 18-sq-km Dal Lake in Srinagar is divided into four basins by raised paths which people can walk on. Along its shores are beautiful Mughal gardens. Its 500 **wooden houseboats** were once summer homes for British officers. Shikaras or smaller wooden boats are a means of transport and fishing.

Ladakh, or the 'land of high passes', lies between the Great Himalayas and the Karakoram ranges, and across the Ladakh and the Zanskar ranges. One of the world's highest motorable passes goes from Leh to Nubra Valley across the Khardung La pass at 18,380 ft.

In Ladakh they believe in Bon, an animistic religion in which the forces of nature are worshipped. Many of its ancient rituals were later merged with Buddhism. Here Gompas or Buddhist monasteries are storehouses of icons, murals and scrolls.

To survive Ladakh's nine months of bitterly cold winter, animals here hibernate, migrate, have more red blood cells, or grow shaggy, warm coats. Annually, many red foxes, snow leopards and stone martens are slaughtered for their fur. In Aksai Chin, the chiru deer is killed to make Shahtoosh shawls.

In the Chiling village of Ladakh, exquisite silver, brass and copper teapots, bowls and hookah bases are made by metal workers. Garas or blacksmiths make large ornate iron stoves. Fabrics like pure Pashmina shawls and pattu or woollen clothing are spun by women on drop-spindles.

Once on the Silk Route between China and the Mediterranean, Ladakh had diverse communities: Indo-Aryan Dards, Buddhist Mons, Tibetans, Central Asian Baltis and the nomadic Changpas. The Namgyal dynasty ruled the region from Leh.

Wild horses, red foxes, ibexes, Tibetan wolves, lynxes, Bactrian camels, brown and black bears, stone martens, wild yaks, snow leopards and Tibetan sand foxes live in Ladakh. The Hemis High Altitude NP has tibetan wolves, shapus, bharals or blue sheep, nyans or the world's largest sheep, and urials, the world's smallest sheep.

Kar-i-kalamdan, or the art of making lacquered pen cases out of paper pulp, grew in the 1400s under Sultan Zain-ul-Abideen. In the 1800s, French agents exported shawls in these delicately painted boxes, and later sold the boxes separately.

In Ladakh, tea is first boiled and then shaken with fresh butter and salt to make butter tea. Butter keeps the body warm, gives energy and prevents chapped lips. The Kashmiri nun or shir chai is a pinkish, salted tea. It is served from a samovar

Kashmir's famous embroidery or Kashida has chinar and grape leaves, cypress cones, flowers and almonds as motifs. Phirans, cloaks, rugs, shawls, linen and bags are covered with chain, buttonhole and cross-filling stitches. Crewel work or wool embroidery is done using hooks on thick namda carpets.

Fact File

Date of formation: October 26, 1947
Size: 2,22,236 sq km
Population: 10,143,700
Capital: Srinagar (in summer) and Jammu (in winter)
Rivers: Chenab, Jhelum, Indus, Zanskar, Suru, Nubra, Shyok
Forests and NPs: Dachigam NP, Hemis High Altitude NP

Languages: Urdu, Hindi, Punjabi, Dogri, Kashmiri, Balti, Ladakhi, Purig, Gurji, Dadri
Neighbours: Himachal Pradesh, Punjab; **International:** Pakistan, Afghanistan, China
State Animal: Hangul
State Bird: Black-necked crane
State Tree: Chinar
State Flower: Lotus

Himachal Pradesh

lies in the high, snow-clad mountains of the Western Himalayas. Known as the 'snow-mountain state', Himachal Pradesh (HP) was once on the Silk Route, with an old road connecting Shimla to the Tibetan border. Work to re-build the ancient 'Hindustan-Tibet Road' began in 1850 under Lord Dalhousie and Sir Charles Napier.

The first settlers here were the **Kols or Mundas**, Nagas, Kinnars and Yakshas, followed by Mongoloid tribes like Bhotias and Kiratas. Last of all, came the Central Asian Aryans. Later, the region had Janapads or republics like the Audumbara republic, which Chandragupta, and later still, Ashoka took over.

After the Guptas, **Harshavardhan** took over. When he died in AD 647, Rajputs ruled here, followed by the Mughals. Maharaj Sansar Chand came into power here after that. The Gorkhas of Nepal conquered some parts after 1768. Lahaul was ruled by Ladakh and Kulu till the 1840s. Sikhs ruled here briefly. After winning the Anglo-Sikh wars, the British established their rule over the region.

Shimla

One of Punjab's important rivers, the **Beas**, originates in the 4631-m-high Rohtang Pass in the Beas Kund. It flows through the Kullu and Kangra valleys to join the Sutlej in Punjab. It was probably called Hyphasis by Alexander's tired army, who refused to go any further east from this point.

Shimla lies 7100 ft above sea level. It was the summer capital of British India. Kullu Valley, Manali and Dalhousie are popular tourist spots.

The **Pin Valley NP** in Spiti is a cold, trans-Himalayan desert where ibexes, blue sheep or bharal, snowcocks, snow partridges and Tibetan snow finches survive. The region, though barren, has lots of fossils. Its many medicinal herbs are used in the Tibetan Amchi form of medicine.

In and around **Manali**, the starting point for the ancient trade route to Ladakh, are places of amazing beauty. Rakshas, or nomadic hunters, once lived here. Manali has many Buddhist monasteries or Gompas.

The **Kullu Valley**, on either side of River Beas, has pine and deodar forests, fruit orchards, glens or deep valleys with water running through them, and beautiful meadows. Kullu also has many ancient temples and is famous for its Dussehra celebrations.

Dharamsala, in the Kangra valley of the Dhauladhar Mountains, has an old history of Hinduism and Buddhism. Tenzin Gyatso—the Dalai Lama—and his followers fled here following Chinese occupation of Tibet in 1959. Upper Dharamsala or McLeodganj is called 'Little Lhasa'.

The boiling hot **Manikaran springs** well up in clusters near the River Parvati in Kullu. Important for religious reasons to both Hindus and Sikhs, the spring water is hot enough to cook rice, dal and vegetables. Vashist village near the Rohtang Pass also has hot sulphur springs.

HP's 32 wildlife sanctuaries and two national parks have 64 mammal, 463 bird and 3240 plant species among them. The Great Himalayan NP has a rich biodiversity—gorals, tahrs, **snow leopards**, serows, brown and black bears, and birds like western tragopans are found here.

The world's oldest democracy is believed to be a tiny, isolated village called **Malana**. Its houses, Kanashi language, customs and governmental structure are all unique, as are the motifs carved into its wooden buildings. Malanis say they were taught their ways by a sage called Jamlu Rishi.

HP has **three mountain ranges** within the Himalayan system—the Shivalik Hills (5000 ft), the Lower Himalayas to the north (15,200 ft), and the Great Himalayas and the Zanskar Mountains (22,000 ft) which lie further still. With trees being cut at an alarming rate, the Shivalik range is slowly losing its soil and ecological diversity.

Samuel Stokes (later called Satyananda) was the only American to be imprisoned during the Indian freedom movement. He came to Shimla in 1904. The Red and Golden Delicious apple saplings he later brought from America gave HP's economy a huge boost. Though apples grew in HP before this, they were sour.

Nicholas Roerich, a Russian painter, travelled with his family through Central Asia and finally settled down in Kullu. He campaigned for the Roerich Pact, under which countries agreed not to bomb each others' cultural monuments. His first son George was a Tibetologist, while the second, Svetoslav, was an artist.

Arts & Crafts

Pahari painting is done in the Basohli and Kangra styles. The Basohli style, popular in the 1600s, used bright colours and strong lines. It originated in Jammu and Kashmir and later spread to HP, where it grew as the Kangra style. Popular from the 1700s, it was refined and used lighter, calmer colours.

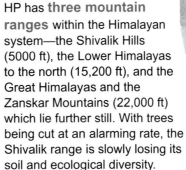

Kinnauri shawls are intricately woven with geometrical motifs. They are usually white, black, grey or brown, with colourful patterns. Kullu shawls are popular, as are the **woollen caps** with geometric-patterned borders, which are worn on special occasions.

The **Chamba Rumal** has Kangra style paintings embroidered on cloth using the delicate double satin stitch or do-rukha which makes the embroidery look the same on both sides. Colourful raw silk threads are stitched on white khadi or muslin 'rumals'. Krishna and Shiva stories, and hunts were popular subjects.

Fact File

Date of formation: January 25, 1971
Size: 55,673 sq km
Population: 60,77,900
Capital: Shimla
Rivers: Ravi, Beas, Chenab, Sutlej, Yamuna
Forests and National Parks: Pin Valley NP, Greater Himalayan NP, Renuka WS, Chail WS, Kalatope Khajjiar WS

Languages: Hindi, Punjabi, Kinnauri, Pahari
Neighbours: **National**: Jammu and Kashmir, Punjab, Haryana, Uttarakhand
International: China
State Animal: Snow leopard
State Bird: Western tragopan
State Tree: Deodar
State Flower: Pink rhododendron

Punjab

Punjab was a part of the Indus Valley Civilisation which grew around the River Sindhu or the Indus. Harappa and Mohenjodaro—now in Pakistan—were two of the many places where traces of the ancient civilisation were found. Sufism thrived in Punjab and Sikhism was born here. The Rig Veda was probably written here.

Five rivers once flowed through Punjab, giving the region its name—'punj' or five, and 'ab' or waters. But after the creation of Pakistan and the separation of Haryana, just two remain—the Beas and the Sutlej. The Shivalik Hills are an important part of the state's geography, as are its foothills and flat alluvial plains.

Sikhism, founded by Guru Nanak, was influenced by Hinduism (the Bhakti, Sant and Nath movements), Islam and Sufism. The word 'Sikh' means a 'learner'. The Sikh holy book, *Adi Granth*, has around 6000 hymns by the 10 Sikh gurus, and saints from all religions and castes. The hymns, set to different ragas, are in Punjabi or Hindi.

Chandigarh

Throughout early history, different armies swooped into Punjab. **Darius I** of Persia conquered it, and around 327 BC, Alexander defeated Raja Paurava (Porus). The Mauryas, Sungas, Guptas and Pushpabhutis also ruled here. Later, Central Asian tribes like Ghoris, Ghaznavids and Mongols attacked Punjab.

Sikh Gurus built many water tanks. Guru Ram Das, the fourth guru built **Amrita Sarovar** or the 'pool of nectar' on land given to him by Akbar. The town of Amritsar grew around it. The fifth Guru, Arjan Sahib, designed and built the Harmandir Sahib temple on an island in the Amrita Sarovar.

Guru Nanak (1469-1539), born in Lahore, composed hymns and travelled extensively—reaching even Mecca by some accounts. Influenced by many great writer-saints (especially Kabir) he founded Sikhism. He was succeeded by nine Gurus. After the tenth, the *Adi Granth* was worshipped as the Guru, or the Granth Sahib.

A blend of Hindu and Muslim architecture, **Harmandir Sahib's** foundation was laid by Mian Mir, a Muslim saint, and it was completed in 1604.

Unlike Hindu temples, it is open on all four sides as a symbol of equality. A gold-foil-covered copper dome was made during Ranjit Singh's rule (giving it its other name: the Golden Temple).

The first person to give Punjab its independence was Banda Singh Bahadur. Sikhs ruled from 1710 to 1849, after which the East India Company took over. **Maharaja Ranjit Singh** (1780-1839) took over his father's 'misl' or territory at 12. He unified Punjab, stopped capital punishment, formed a powerful army and ran a secular government. The kingdom collapsed after his death.

Most of Punjab's forests were cleared for farming and industrial growth. But there are **protected areas and sanctuaries** like Bir Moti Bagh, Bir Bhunerhari, Bir Dosanjh, Bir Bhadson, Bir Mehas, Bir Gurdialpura and Takhni Rehmapur. They have blackbucks, leopards, jungle cats, nilgais and rhesus macaques.

Punjabi dances are energetic and graceful. The bhangra, luddi, julli, jaago, dhamal and jhumar are performed by men; while women dance the gidda and the sammi. The Gidda, accompanied by 'bolis' or funny songs, was supposedly taught to women by Giddho, a fairy. The Sammi is still performed by some tribes.

Sufism, a mystical form of Islam, believes in a philosophy of love and universal oneness. Khwaja Moinuddin Chisti, a Sufi, came here in the 1100s. Later, Sufi poets like Baba Farid, Shah Hussain, Sultan Bahu, Waris Shah and others wrote in Punjabi. In the 1700s, Bulle Shah wrote poetry full of love for humanity and Punjab.

The Non-Cooperation Movement of 1920-1922 was spurred on by a horrifying massacre on April 13, 1919, Baisakhi day, at **Jallianwala Bagh** in Amritsar. General Dyer fired on an unarmed group of protestors, killing and injuring thousands. A memorial stands at the site today.

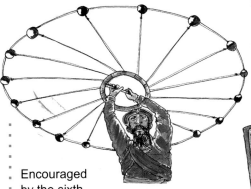

Punjabi music has khayal, thumri, ghazal, qawwali and Sikh hymns. The Patiala Gharana was started by Ustad Jasae Khan in the 1800s, followed by Ditae Khan and Kalu Khan. Among its famous exponents are Bade Ghulam Ali Khan, Ghulam Ali, Farida Khanum, Lakshmi Shankar, Nirmala Devi and Ajoy Chakravorty.

Encouraged by the sixth Sikh Guru Hargobind, wrestling was seen as a way to prepare the body for battle. Cart-racing, tent-pegging, archery, fencing, gymnastics and acrobatics by the **Nihangs** (an armed order of Sikhs) and kabaddi and khido khoondi are popular at rural Punjab's sports meets.

Wetlands or marshes are protected for their biodiversity. **Harike wetland** has rare testudine turtles, smooth Indian otters, diving ducks and falcated teals. With their rich ecosystems, the Harike, Kanjli and Ropar wetlands here are called Wetlands of International Importance, or **Ramsar Sites**.

Arts & Crafts

Phulkari or 'flower embroidery' was done on brick-red coarse hand-spun cloth. Chinese or Afghan silk yarn that was dyed in Jammu or Amritsar was used for the stitches. Women did the darning stitch to fill the fabric with profuse embroidery in bright yellow, orange, crimson and white. While most phulkari shawls have embroidered sides, the bagh or 'garden' shawl is entirely covered with the jewel-bright stitch.

Punjab's many wood-work centres like Jalandhar, Amritsar and Bhera are known for their dexterous carving. The **wood inlay** of Hoshiarpur on black shisham wood is famous for its detailed Mughal, animal, floral and geometrical designs. Traditionally, ivory was used in the inlay, but now plastic, old piano keys and even zinc are used.

Fact File

Date of formation: January 26, 1950
Size: 50,362 sq km
Population: 2,43,58,999
Capital: Chandigarh
Rivers: Beas, Sutlej, Ravi
Forests and NPs: Bir Moti Bagh, Bir Bhunerhari, Bir Dosanjh
Language: Punjabi

Neighbours: **National**: Jammu and Kashmir, Himachal Pradesh, Haryana, Rajasthan; **International**: Pakistan
State Animal: Blackbuck
State Bird: Eastern goshawk
State Tree: Shisham

Haryana

Haryana shares its capital—Chandigarh—with Punjab. Parts of it are highly fertile and though rain is scanty, it is well-irrigated with canals. An inscription in Sanskrit dating from AD 1328 found here calls the region 'Hariana' or 'god's abode'.

Lying on the route that most invading tribes took to enter India, Haryana was the birthplace of **early Hinduism**. Aryan settlers wrote and formulated Vedic hymns and manuscripts here. Kurukshetra here was the site of the mythical Mahabharata war, where Krishna revealed the Bhagavad Gita to his friend, Arjuna.

Many invaders like the **Huns** and Alexander's army swept through Haryana. The three historic battles of Panipat were fought here: in 1526 between Babur and Ibrahim Lodi, in 1556 between Akbar and Hemu, and in 1761 between Ahmad Shah Durrani and the Marathas.

Fossils of prehistoric mammals from the Plio-pleistocene period 2.5 million years ago were found near the Shivaliks, in an area now known as the Saketi Fossil Park. The Geographical Survey of India has made fibre-glass models of the extinct **giant land tortoises** and **four-horned giraffes** that once roamed here.

Chandigarh

Haryana has **four major geographical regions**: the plain formed by the Rivers Yamuna and Ghaggar; the Shivalik hills in the north; the semi-desert plain on the Rajasthan border; and the Aravalli range to the south.

Haryana used to be a part of Punjab, but when Indian states were divided on linguistic grounds, both Sikhs and Hindus demanded single-language states. Actually, demands for Haryana's statehood were made even before 1947, by freedom fighters like Asaf Ali and Lala Lajpat Rai.

Haryana is **highly industrialised**, with a network of agriculture-based industries like those involved in making farm machinery, processing farm products and the bicycle industry. Gurgaon and Faridabad are commercial and industrial centres.

Jats are Haryana's farming community. Fertile Haryana was aggressively cultivated during the Green Revolution with canal irrigation, high-yield seeds and fertilisers. It has many wealthy farmers and contributes greatly to India's food and milk production.

Legend has it that **Panipat** was once full of flies which Saint Bu Ali Shah Qalandar got rid of. Ibrahim Lodi was defeated here by Babur. Lodi's tomb, Bu Ali Shah's tomb, the Kabuli Shah Mosque, and the Salar Jung Gate are important landmarks.

Haryanvi dances are energetic. Among others are the girls-only Loor performed during Holi; the pre-harvest, moonlight Ahir dance called Dhamal; the women-only Jhumar; the Phag (set to instruments like the tasha and nagada); and the Ghoomar by women along the Rajasthan border.

A dense sal forest in the foothills of the Shivaliks, **Kalesar forest** was formally declared an NP in 2003. Kalesar has leopards, panthers, hares, sambhars, red junglefowls, chitals, porcupines, brahminy ducks, mallards and elephants.

Faridabad was named after Emperor Jahangir's treasurer, Sheikh Farid, who built it in 1607. Lake Badhkal in the Aravallis, is now mostly dry because of blockages by mines. Lake Surajkund was a reservoir built by the Tomar King Surajpal.

Holi is celebrated here in spring, Lohri in winter, Baisakhi in summer, Teej in monsoon, and Sanjhi in October. **Gugga Naumi** is observed by both Hindus and Muslims. It honours Gugga Pir who could cure snake bites. Devotees dance in a procession with instruments like thalis and chimtas.

The 359-acre Sultanpur NP and Bird Sanctuary near Gurgaon has nearly 250 resident bird species and about 100 migratory ones. Lake Sultanpur's potential as a sanctuary was spotted by the ornithologist Peter Jackson. Purple sunbirds, Eurasian thick-knees, Indian crested larks, red-vented bulbuls and **black francolins** are found here.

Arts & Crafts

In Haryana and Punjab, women and entire families make shoes called **tilla or kasuri juttis** from buffalo and goat hide. Traditionally, the shoes came in colours like deep red, black and tan. Nowadays gold, silk and metal threads, beads and coloured leather strips are also added.

In villages bordering Rajasthan, Himachal Pradesh and Punjab, many women weave **panja dhurries**. A frame is made on a traditional cot. The warp yarns (lengthwise) are stretched on it, and the weaver works in the weft yarns (horizontal). A claw-like 'panja' is used to tighten the yarns after each weft yarn is woven in.

Fact File

Date of formation: November 1, 1966
Size: 44,212 sq km
Population: 21,144,564
Capital: Chandigarh
Rivers: Yamuna, Ghaggar
Forests and NPs: Sultanpur NP, Kalesar NP, Simbalawara WS
Languages: Hindi, Punjabi, Urdu

Neighbours: Punjab, Chandigarh, Himachal Pradesh, Uttar Pradesh, Uttarakhand, Delhi, Rajasthan
State Animal: Blackbuck
State Bird: Black francolin
State Tree: Peepal
State Flower: Lotus

Uttarakhand

or the 'northern section', has high mountains and glaciers, which are the sources of great rivers. Many Hindu epics were either written or set here. Uttarakhand's vegetation and climate vary at different heights—it has icy glaciers in the north and tropical forests in the south. Two important rivers originate here: the Ganga and the Yamuna.

The **Kol-Munds** (a Dravidian people) were probably the first to live here; the Nagas, Khasas, Hunas, Kiratas, Gujars and Aryans came in later. Dynasties like the Pauravas, Kushanas, Kunindas, Guptas, Katyuris, Palas, Chands and Parmaras ruled here.

Dehradun was set up when Aurangzeb gave Baba Ram Rai—the seventh Sikh Guru's son who founded a breakaway sect—a jagir or gift of land in a 'Dun' or 'small valley'. 'Dehra', another word for a camp, took its name from Ram Rai's settlement.

Glaciers or bomaks—large, frozen, slow-moving masses of ice—are often the sources of rivers. Gangotri, Gaumukh, the Nanda Devi group, Pindari, Tipra, Satopanth and Milam glaciers are awe-inspiring and ecologically important.

Dehradun

To ancient Hindus, Garhwal and Kumaon were known as **Kedarkhand and Manaskhand**. The demand for a separate state of Uttarakhand (the Puranic name for the central Himalayas) began in the 1950s. The state was carved out of Uttar Pradesh in 2000 and called 'Uttaranchal' against popular opinion. It was renamed 'Uttarakhand' in 2007.

Garhwal and Kumaon were traditional enemies. A lot of Hindu mythology is set in **Garhwal**. Garhwal was once part of the Mauryan Empire and had 52 small kingdoms with garhs or forts. King Ajai Pal is credited with having unified it in the 1300s.

Badrinath, dedicated to Vishnu, sits between the Nar and Narayan mountain ranges. It is at the source of the River Alaknanda and wild berries or 'badri' once lined its floor. The temple was built in the 8th century AD by Adi Shankaracharya, the reformer from Kerala.

? Stone Age man lived in Kumaon and left **Mesolithic** era paintings in the rock shelters of **Lakhu Udyar**. The Katyuri kings who ruled here (7th to 11th centuries AD) built the 900-year-old Katarmal Sun Temple. They used stone instead of bricks to build. Later, the Chands of Pithoragarh built a complex of 124 temples in Jageshwar.

In Kumaon, pre-Hindu **folk deities** like village, land, snake, family gods, and Veers or heroes are worshiped and poems or Jagars praise them. Naina Devi, Nanda Devi, Bholanath (the ghost of a Chand prince), Haru (a Veer), Gangnath (a murdered lover), Airy and Chamu are among them.

Kedarnath temple, at a height of 3584 m, is devoted to Shiva. It is at the source of River Mandakini. The original temple is said to have been built by the Pandavas. It was probably re-built by Adi Shankaracharya in the 8th century AD.

The Ganga originates at Gaumukh in the Gangotri glacier 10,300 ft above sea level. It travels down 253 km to enter the Indo-Gangetic plain of north India at **Haridwar**. The Magh Melas are held here every year, the Ardha Kumbh Mela every six years, and the Kumbh Mela every 12.

Arts & Crafts

Arts & Crafts

Three sanctuaries near the Shivaliks were merged to create **Rajaji NP** in 1983. It has 400 bird species, wild elephants, tigers, leopards, sambhars, chitals and fossils of prehistoric animals and plants.

Contractors cut trees in Chamoli causing deforestation and depriving villagers of their income. In 1973, village women hugged trees to protect them from axes in a movement called **Chipko**. Sundarlal Bahuguna, a Gandhian activist, campaigned with Chipko to preserve forests and rivers. He walked 5000 km across the Himalayas and gave Chipko its slogan: Ecology is permanent economy.

Traditionally, houses all over Uttarakhand had beautifully carved wooden doors and panels. Flowers, hills, fish, fruits, people and birds were carved into the wood. Known as kholi, the resplendent woodcarving at the doorway showed how prosperous the family was.

Corbett NP in the Terai region was named after **Jim Corbett**, a hunter-conservationist who shot man-eating tigers but also understood the need to conserve them and their habitats. The Valley of Flowers NP has meadows with 300 species of tall wild flowers. It is a part of the Nanda Devi **Biosphere Reserve**. The Reserve and the Valley are **World Heritage Sites**.

Aipan, or rangoli, has great religious significance, with specific designs being used for different occasions. Naming ceremonies, thread ceremonies, weddings—all have the distinct white-on-red aipans being drawn at the main door or in the courtyard.

Fact File

Date of formation: November 9, 2000
Size: 53,484 sq km
Population: 84,89,349
Capital: Dehradun
Rivers: Ganga, Yamuna, Ramganga, Kali
Forests and NPs: Nanda Devi NP, Rajaji NP, Corbett Tiger Reserve

Languages: Hindi, Garhwali, Kumaoni
Neighbours: National: Himachal Pradesh, Uttar Pradesh
International: China
State Animal: Himalayan musk deer
State Bird: Himalayan monal
State Tree: Burans
State Flower: Brahm kamal

Uttar Pradesh

is where Buddhist sculpture, Mughal art and architecture, and the kathak dance form developed. Aryans settled in the Doab region and called it Aryavarta or Bharatavarsha, after Bharata, one of their powerful kings. Uttar Pradesh (UP) was given its current name by Govind Vallabh Pant, its first chief minister.

UP's history had **five major periods**: the prehistoric (till 600 BC), the Buddhist-Hindu (600 BC to AD 1200), the Muslim and Mughal (1200-1775), the British (1775-1947), and the post-independence period. The *Ramayana* was set in Ayodhya, in the Mahajanapad or republic of Kosala. The *Mahabharata* was set in Hastinapur in western UP.

The ancient Dhamek **Stupa** marks the spot where Buddha gave his first sermon in Sarnath. The powerful Maurya (320-300 BC), Kushan (AD 100-250) and Gupta (AD 320-415) empires controlled UP. The **four-lion Ashoka pillar**, later the Indian government's emblem, was installed here to mark Ashoka's visit.

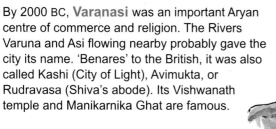

Lucknow ◉

By the end of the 1100s, Muhammed of Ghur defeated the Gahadavalas. Many Muslim dynasties ruled UP, but the **Mughal dynasty**, set up by Babur when he defeated Ibrahim Lodi in 1526, was the most vibrant. During its 200-year rule, music, art, dance and architecture flowered.

Hindi and Urdu are forms of Khariboli. Urdu developed when local dialects merged with Arabic, Persian and Turkish. The Turkish word 'ordu' meant 'army', and since the dialect was used by soldiers, it was called 'Urdu' or Lashkari Zubaan. Urdu slowly replaced Persian as the official language of Lucknow's court.

Beginning in south India, the Bhakti or devotional movement reached the north. Ramananda (1400-1470), its founder there, felt that a person's caste or class did not matter. He wrote in Hindi, so that his work could be read by everyone. His student, **Kabir**, believed in a formless god and in the unity of all religions. Kabir's dohas (rhymed couplets) were collected in the *Granth Sahib*.

By 2000 BC, **Varanasi** was an important Aryan centre of commerce and religion. The Rivers Varuna and Asi flowing nearby probably gave the city its name. 'Benares' to the British, it was also called Kashi (City of Light), Avimukta, or Rudravasa (Shiva's abode). Its Vishwanath temple and Manikarnika Ghat are famous.

Soldiers of the Bengal army revolted in Meerut on May 10, 1857, sparking off India's first war of independence. Most of the rebels—Muslims and Hindus—were from UP. The Maratha queen **Rani Lakshmi bai** of Jhansi fought bravely alongside warriors like Gulam Ghaus Khan, Moti bai, Jhalkari bai, Lala Bhau Bakshi and others.

Jallaluddin Akbar (1542-1605) was a wise emperor. His philosophy, Din-i-Ilahi, brought together different religions. When he had a son, he built a magnificent red-sandstone city in the town of Sikri to thank Sheikh Salim Chisti who had blessed him. Called **Fatehpur Sikri**, it was the Mughal capital for about 10 years, after which it was abandoned. It is now a World Heritage Site.

When Mumtaz Mahal died in 1631, the heart-broken Emperor Shah Jahan built the hauntingly beautiful **Taj Mahal**. The tomb took 22 years, 20,000 labourers and many experts to build. It is a World Heritage Site.

Allahabad or ancient Prayag was an Aryan settlement at the meeting point of Rivers Ganga, Yamuna and the mythical Saraswati. Akbar founded it in 1583 as 'Al-Ilahabad' or the City of God. The Kumbh Mela is held here every 12 years.

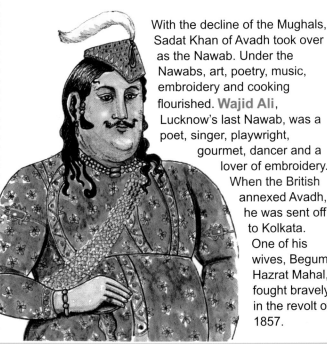

The River Ganga is frighteningly polluted, endangering the people who live by it, and its small, nearly-blind **gangetic dolphins**. The Sankat Mochan Foundation—led by Dr Veer Bhadra Mishra, an engineer and a priest—tries to clean the river and educate people.

With the decline of the Mughals, Sadat Khan of Avadh took over as the Nawab. Under the Nawabs, art, poetry, music, embroidery and cooking flourished. **Wajid Ali**, Lucknow's last Nawab, was a poet, singer, playwright, gourmet, dancer and a lover of embroidery. When the British annexed Avadh, he was sent off to Kolkata. One of his wives, Begum Hazrat Mahal, fought bravely in the revolt of 1857.

South of Nepal and north of UP is a marshy grassland stretching from the Yamuna in the west to the Brahmaputra in the east. Called **Terai**, or 'moist land', the area has Savannah type grasslands which are among the tallest in the world. Terai is also linked to the Duars and stretches into Nepal. Above the marshy stretches are bhabars or stretches of gravel and pebbles.

Arts & Crafts

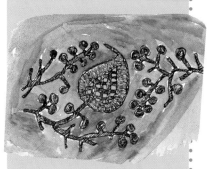

Lucknow is famous for **Chikankari**, a craft that the Nawabs loved. In Persian, Chikan means 'cloth made of needle-work'. Chikan, also called shadow-work embroidery, is done on fine muslin. Murri, bakhia, jaali, tepchi, dhum and kato are among the 36 different Chikan stitches.

Banarasi brocades are woven with different coloured silk threads. Sometimes zari or silver and gold threads are also used. There are three kinds of brocades: zari (kimkhabs and potthans), amru (tanchois) and abrawan (tarbana). Naqshabandhs drew the designs which were woven into these rich fabrics.

Sanjhi, the 17th century art of cutting paper stencils, was a form of worship. While men practised the art in temples, the folk version was done by girls. The motifs usually came from the *Ras Leela*. Later Mughal motifs like the jaali or lattice, animals and flowers were used.

Fact File

- **Date of formation:** January 26, 1950
  Size: 2,40,928 km
  Population: 1,66,052,859
  Capital: Lucknow
- **Rivers:** Ganga, Yamuna, Gomti, Ghaghra, Ramganga, Betwa
  Forests and NPs: Dudhwa NP, Corbett NP, Kedarnath WS, Govind WS
- **Languages:** Hindi, Urdu

Neighbours: National: Uttarakhand, Himachal Pradesh, Haryana, Delhi, Rajasthan, Madhya Pradesh, Chhattisgarh, Jharkhand, Bihar
International: Nepal
State Animal: Swamp deer
State Bird: Sarus crane
State Tree: Ashok
State Flower: Brahm kamal

Rajasthan

is full of surprising contrasts. It is divided diagonally by the Aravalli Mountains, so that the northwest is a stark desert, while the southeast is fertile and hilly. People wear bright, cheerful colours, creating a stunning contrast with the arid brown desert. In fact, entire Rajasthani cities are painted in bright, unique colours.

Traces of the ancient **Harappan civilisation** were found in parts of Rajasthan. From around 200 BC, Bactrian Greeks, Sakas or Scythians, Guptas, Huns and Harshavardhan ruled here. Between AD 600 and 1000, different Rajput dynasties like the Gurjara-Pratiharas, Guhilas, Chauhans, Kachwahas, Bhattis and Rathods were in power here.

In the older parts of Jaipur, the 'pink city', buildings are actually painted pink! Jaipur was built in 1727 by Maharaja Sawai Jai Singh II, a passionate astronomer. Of the five observatories he built, the largest was Jaipur's **Jantar Mantar**.

Jaipur ◉

Rajput power rose to its peak in the 1500s under **Rana Sangram Singh**, who was later vanquished by Babur. By the end of the 1500s, Akbar, who fought the Rajputs, also forged ties of marriage with them. After Aurangazeb died in 1707, the Jats and then the Marathas took over. The British ruled here from the 1800s.

Keoladeo Ghana NP, a World Heritage Site, has saras cranes, egrets, herons, kingfishers and geese. A bund or dam was made here in 1726. Later, more water was diverted here to draw birds for shooting. It was declared an NP in 1981. Rare Siberian cranes used to fly down for winters, and once 200 were spotted. Their numbers have dropped now.

Tucked away between the Aravalli and the Vindhya mountains, **Ranthambore NP** has tigers, 300 bird species, a dense forest, ancient temples, mosques, and a 10th century fort. It is one of **Project Tiger's** most challenging and successful reserves.

The **Sariska Tiger Reserve** was established in 1978 under Project Tiger. Inside Sariska is a fort, and at its edge is Bhangarh, a ghost town, uninhabited since the 1600s! Though it was said that there were 18 tigers in Sariska, in 2005 conservationists found that there were probably none left here.

TIGERS ?

Rajasthan has many religious, festive and animal fairs with dances, strange competitions and fireworks. Fairs in Pushkar, Nagaur, Gangaur, Jaipur, Bikaner and Baneshwar's tribal fair are famous. Jaipur's **Elephant Festival** has a tug-of-war between humans and elephants.

Shekhawati was on the trade route between coastal towns and the interior of the country. Its rich traders built havelis and painted huge frescoes on the walls, depicting gods, historical events or huge animals.

Rajasthani **miniature paintings** were made using gold and stone colours, and squirrel-hair brushes on cloth, paper or silk. Kangra, Jodhpur, Jaipur, Mewar and Mughal are the different 'schools' or styles.

Ranakpur, a complex of Jain temples, lies in a valley of the Aravallis. The entire complex is carved out of marble, and has 1444 distinctly carved pillars. No two are alike.

. . . .

Sonar Qila, a fort made of yellow sandstone, was built by Rawal Jaisal in 1156, when he founded Jaisalmer, the 'yellow city'. Because too many people live inside the fort, it has become an endangered monument.

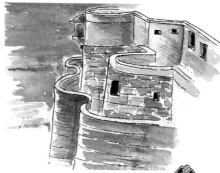

In Jaipur and Udaipur, **Pichhvai** paintings were done on cloth and hung behind temple idols. In Bhilwara, Phad or large, vibrant scroll paintings tell stories of local heroes like Pabuji. Minstrels called bhopas sing of their valour.

Jodhpur, founded in 1459 by Rao Jodha, has some beautiful cenotaphs or memorial **chhatris**. The indigo blue colour of the houses here is said to repel mosquitoes. Dhawa WS nearby has the most number of Indian antelopes.

Kathputlis or string puppets are made by the Bhat community, who travel and perform with them. They have wooden heads with big, expressive features. The rest of the body is made up of a loose, pleated skirt. Only horse-rider puppets have legs.

The **hand-block printing** of Rajasthan uses motifs like scorpions, centipedes, creepers, chillies, birds, leaves, ladders and elephants. Colours, motifs and methods change with towns and communities.

Bikaner was founded by Rao Bika in 1488. It has red sandstone havelis and Jain temples. In the **Karni Mata temple** here, rats are worshipped.

In Rajasthan—the only Indian state with a desert—water is precious. **Panihari music** is made up of the folksongs sung by women as they walk to wells to draw and bring water home.

fact file

- **Date of formation**: November 1, 1956
  Size: 3,42,239 sq km
  Population: 56,473,122
  Capital: Jaipur
- **Rivers**: Luni, Banas, Kali Sindh, Chambal
  Forests and NPs: Sariska Tiger Reserve, Keoladeo Ghana NP, Ranthambore NP, Dhawa WS

Languages: Rajasthani, Hindi
Neighbours: **National**: Gujarat, Madhya Pradesh, Uttar Pradesh, Delhi, Haryana, Punjab
International: Pakistan
State Animal: Chinkara
State Bird: Great Indian bustard
State Tree: Khejri
State Flower: Rohira

Bihar

Bihar gets its name from the Sanskrit word 'vihara' or 'abode', referring to the many Buddhist monasteries found here. Gautama Buddha achieved enlightenment here, as did Mahavira, the founder of Jainism. Bihar has witnessed many changes—religious, artistic and imperial—that swept through India.

One of the world's oldest capitals, **Patna** was called Kusumpura, Pushpapura, Pataliputra and Azeemabad by different rulers. Set in an arch along the Ganga, its history begins with Ajatashatru who built a fort called Pataligram here in the 5th century BC. His son Udaya moved his capital here from the older Rajgir.

Between 600 BC and 321 BC, in the late Vedic period, Bihar had 16 states or republics called **Mahajanapadas** which were ruled by a council of kings or elders. The Buddha probably based the working of the Sangha or monastic order on that of Vrijji, one of the world's first republics. One state, Magadha, grew powerful. The Mauryas, its rulers, conquered much of India.

Later, between the 4th and the 5th century AD, the **Guptas** ruled Magadha. Pala rule followed from 775 till 1200. From about 1200 to 1765, it was under Muslim rulers, like Sher Shah Suri. The British ruled here from 1765.

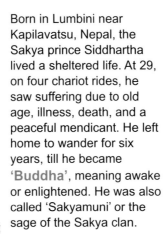

Patna

Born in Lumbini near Kapilavatsu, Nepal, the Sakya prince Siddhartha lived a sheltered life. At 29, on four chariot rides, he saw suffering due to old age, illness, death, and a peaceful mendicant. He left home to wander for six years, till he became **'Buddha'**, meaning awake or enlightened. He was also called 'Sakyamuni' or the sage of the Sakya clan.

Prince Vardhamana, born in Vaishali into the Nata clan around 599 BC, gave up worldly life at 30, and became known as **Mahavira**. The last of the 24 Tirthankaras or Jain gurus, Mahavira systematised Jain beliefs, laying down rules for ordinary people, monks and nuns.

Nalanda University—a Mahavihara or seat of Buddhist learning—was founded around the 5th century AD. Hsuan-Tsang, the Chinese scholar, studied here in the 7th century. Nalanda blossomed under the Palas, between the 8th and 12th centuries. Indian scientific and cultural knowledge was also taught here.

A peepal or **Bodhi tree** in Bodh Gaya marks the spot where the Buddha achieved enlightenment. Near it stands a small shrine built by Emperor Ashoka. The 180-ft-high, lean, pyramid-like Mahabodhi temple—a World Heritage Site today—was built in the 2nd century AD during Kushan rule.

Sher Shah Suri (1486-1545), born in Sasaram in Bihar, was of Afghan descent. An enlightened ruler, he introduced a postal system, custom duties and a uniform system of coinage with coins like Rupiya, Mohur and Dam minted to exact weight specifications. He built the Grand Trunk road from Kolkata to Peshawar. His tomb is a striking example of Afghan architecture in India.

Bihar is divided by the Ganga into north and south plains. Gandak, Ghaghara, Baghmati Mahananda and Kosi in the north, and the Son in the south are its tributaries. A flooded Kosi caused much destruction in 2008.

Rajgir WS, located amidst small hills, has hot sulphur springs, wild bears, peafowls, quails, hornbills and partridges. It was the ancient capital of Bihar. King Bimbisara gave Venuvana—a bamboo grove—to the Buddha, making it the first Buddhist monastery ever. King Bimbisara was imprisoned here by his son Ajatashatru.

The Valmiki WS, India's 18th tiger reserve, is 544 sq km. It borders Nepal's Chitwan NP. Often animals like the one-horned rhinoceros and Indian bison migrate from one NP into the other. Also to be found here is the Valmiki ashram, where Sage Valmiki is believed to have composed the *Ramayana.*

In Bihar they speak languages like Bhojpuri, Maithili, Magadhi, Hindi and Urdu. Maithili is an ancient language with literature of its own, written using a script called Tirhuta or Mithilakshar. Munda, Santhal and Ho tribes speak languages from the Austroasiatic family, while the Oraons speak Kurukh, a Dravidian language.

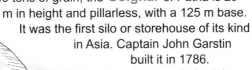

Shaped like a stupa and meant to store nearly 14,000 tons of grain, the Golghar of Patna is 29 m in height and pillarless, with a 125 m base. It was the first silo or storehouse of its kind in Asia. Captain John Garstin built it in 1786. Porters climbed the 145-step spiral staircase along one side and dumped grains in through the hole at the top.

Arts & Crafts

Mithila or Madhubani painting was done on auspicious occasions by women on walls (bhitti) or floors (aripan) using gum, bamboo slivers or matchsticks. William and Mildred Archer first documented the art in the 1930s. When a drought hit Mithila in the 1960s, Pupul Jayakar and Bhaskar Kulkarni suggested that paintings be made on paper and sold.

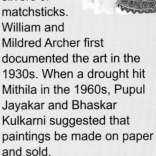

Madhubani's marsh grass is used to make baskets, boxes, toys, dolls, deities and bangles. The golden sikki grass is cut, dried, sliced, shaved and coiled tightly onto a base made of the stronger and cheaper munj grass or raffia.

The Sujini kantha embroidery of Bihar was done by women. They would fold old saris and dhotis together and embroider them into quilts for their children. Sujini uses the running stitch to fill up its motifs. The outline is done using the chain stitch.

Fact File

Date of formation: January 26, 1950
Size: 94,163 sq km
Population: 82,998,509
Capital: Patna
Rivers: Kosi, Ganga, Saryu, Gandak, Kamla, Panar, Saura, Pun-pun
Forests and NPs: Valmiki NP, Rajgir WS, Bhimbandh WS, Gautam Buddha WS, Udayapur WS

Languages: Hindi, Urdu, Santhali
Neighbours: National: Jharkhand, Uttar Pradesh, West Bengal
International: Nepal
State Animal: Gaur
State Bird: Indian roller
State Tree: Peepal
State Flower: Kachnar

Jharkhand

gets its name from the Sanskrit word 'jharikhanda', meaning a thick forest. Located in the Chhota Nagpur plateau, it has dense forests full of sal trees. Nearly **40%** of India's mineral wealth—iron ore, coal, manganese, bauxite and lime—is found here.

Legend has it that the Orissan Raja Jai Singh Deo ruled Jharkhand around the 13th century. For centuries, **Munda Rajas** or tribal kings also ruled here. When the Mughals ruled here, the region was called Kukara. It came to be known as Jharkhand when the British took over in 1765.

North Jharkhand was once part of the ancient Magadha Empire, while the south was under **Kalinga** or Orissa. Jharkhand's rich iron deposits were prized even then for making weapons. Though traditionally considered a part of Bihar, Jharkhand has had a distinct cultural identity from around the time of Bihar's ancient Mahajanapadas or great republics.

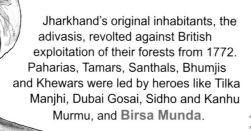

Ranchi

The first voice for a separate tribal state to be formed in southern Bihar was raised by **Jaipal Singh**, the Oxford-educated captain of the Indian hockey team to the 1928 Olympics. After years of struggle, the Parliament passed the Bihar Reorganisation Bill (2000) to carve out 18 districts of Bihar and form Jharkhand, the 28th state of the Indian Republic.

Jharkhand's original inhabitants, the adivasis, revolted against British exploitation of their forests from 1772. Paharias, Tamars, Santhals, Bhumjis and Khewars were led by heroes like Tilka Manjhi, Dubai Gosai, Sidho and Kanhu Murmu, and **Birsa Munda**.

The Ho (1820-1827) and Munda (1831-1832) uprisings were important revolts against the British. The massive **Tana Bhagat Movement** of 1914 merged with Mahatma Gandhi's Civil Disobedience Movement.

Santhals, the largest tribal group here, are a casteless society with a form of self-governance called Manjhi-Pargana. Santhal music is distinctive with instruments like the tamak and tumdak drums, flutes, **dhodro banam** or a one-stringed bowed lute, and phet banam or a multi-stringed, bowed lute.

Betla or Palamau NP is home to 170 bird species, 39 mammals, 17 bamboo species and two ancient Chero dynasty forts. It also has bisons, langurs, rhesus monkeys, blue bulls or nilgai, honey badgers, **pangolins**, tigers and elephants. The world's first tiger census was done here in 1932 by counting pugmarks. Betla became part of Project Tiger in 1974.

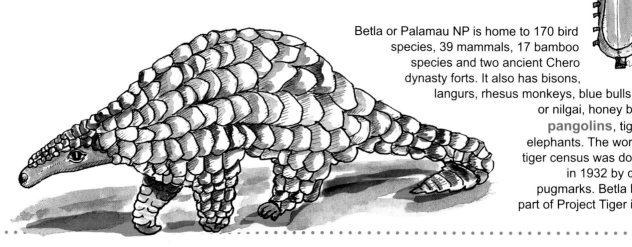

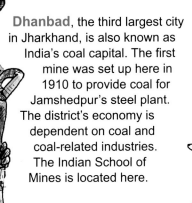

Dhanbad, the third largest city in Jharkhand, is also known as India's coal capital. The first mine was set up here in 1910 to provide coal for Jamshedpur's steel plant. The district's economy is dependent on coal and coal-related industries. The Indian School of Mines is located here.

In Jharkhand they celebrate **farming and nature**. Cattle are washed and worshipped during Sohrai; the sal tree is worshipped during Sarhul; Bhagta parab celebrates spring; Hal punhya marks the beginning of ploughing; and Tusu celebrates the winter harvest.

Jharkhand's 30 or so tribes speak languages from **three different families**: Indo-Aryan languages like Bhojpuri, Nagpuri, Sadri, Hindi, Urdu, Oriya and Bengali; Munda languages like Kurmali, Santhali, Mundari, Bhumij and Ho; and Dravidian languages like Korwa, Kurukh and Paharia.

When **Jamshedji Tata** was looking for a site for India's first steel plant, geologists identified a village here called Sakchi. The steel plant was opened in 1911. Later the site was developed into a township with a tinplate mill, a brick-making plant, a hospital, homes for workers, wide streets, playgrounds and places of worship. Lord Chelmsford named the city 'Jamshedpur' in 1919 in honour of its founder.

Arts & Crafts

Chaitra parab is celebrated with the Chhau Nach in Seraikella. Practised in Jharkhand, Chhattisgarh, West Bengal and Orissa, Chhau is accompanied by wordless music. Dancers wear large, **colourful masks** which are made using dark clay from the banks of the River Kharkai. They are painted with bold lines to give each character a set, symbolic expression.

Jadu patua is a form of scroll painting. A story-teller, who is also a painter and magician, travels with Mritu pat or 'death scrolls', describing to his audience the torment their dead relatives are going through. When they give him money and gifts, the 'troubles' vanish.

Fact File

Date of formation: November 15, 2000
Size: 79,714 sq km
Population: 26,909,428
Capital: Ranchi
Rivers: Damodar, Subarnarekha
Forests and NPs: Betla (Palamau) NP, Hazaribagh WS
Languages: Hindi, Urdu, Santhali

Neighbours: Bihar, Chhattisgarh, Uttar Pradesh, Bengal, Orissa
State Animal: Elephant
State Bird: Asian koel
State Tree: Sal
State Flower: Palash

West Bengal

West Bengal stretches all the way from the Himalayas down to the Bay of Bengal. It is nearly 320 km wide at some parts, and barely 16 km at others. It has a variety of climate types, flora and fauna: the dense marshes of the Sunderbans in the south, paddy fields in the centre, and the cold Himalayan Darjeeling in the north. What it also has, are an array of arts, crafts, literature, music—and sweets!

Bengal was **partitioned** in 1947. West Bengal stayed with India, while the eastern part went to Pakistan. There was a massive flow of refugees on both sides. Later, in 1971, East Pakistan fought for freedom from West Pakistan and became 'Bangladesh'.

An artist, poet, novelist, playwright, composer, and writer of short stories, **Rabindranath Tagore** (1861-1941) had a deep sympathy for the poor. He was the first Asian to win the Nobel Prize for Literature in 1913. He composed the anthems of Bangladesh and India, and songs called Rabindra Sangeet.

Bengal was part of the Maurya kingdom in the 3rd century BC. Around the 4th century AD, it was part of Samudra Gupta's empire, and later, came under Pala rule. From the 1200s till 1757, Bengal was under independent Muslim rulers and sometimes, the Mughals. Bengal's last independent ruler, Nawab Siraj-ud-Daulah, and his French allies were defeated in the battle of **Palashi** (or Plassey) in 1757.

Kolkata

Kolkata was once the capital of British India. It grew from three villages identified by Job Charnok in 1690. Set by the River Hooghly, it was an important port. It has large annual book fairs, monuments like the Victoria Memorial, and grand annual Durga Puja celebrations.

Bengali literature developed early, thanks to the cultural awakening brought about by the Brahmo Samaj. Upendrakishore Roy (1863-1915) collected folklore, wrote on science, pioneered engraving in India and composed music. His son, Sukumar Ray, wrote witty poems (his *Abol-Tabol* is famous), and started *Sandesh,* a children's magazine.

Though he was trained as a fine artist in the Western style, by the late 1920s **Jamini Roy** (1887-1972) created an original and truly independent Indian style of painting. He made vegetable colours and used elements from Bengal's folk art like Santhal, Tantric and Kalighat paintings to recapture the energy of India's folk traditions.

Baul, a musical tradition and a religion, is a blend of Hindu, Islamic, Buddhist and Tantric philosophies. Lalon Fakir (1774–1890) was a famous Baul. Baul music was declared a Masterpiece of the Oral and Intangible Heritage of Humanity by UNESCO. It has influenced writers like Rabindranath Tagore, Kazi Nazrul Islam and Alan Ginsberg.

Ram Mohan Roy (1772-1833) spoke Sanskrit, Arabic, Persian, Hebrew, English and Greek. Influenced by Islam and Christianity, he tried to rid Hinduism of superstition, casteism, idol worship and child marriage. He founded the Brahmo Samaj in 1828, merging Hindu spirituality with Islamic and Christian beliefs. He tried to abolish Sati, the practice of burning widows for their property.

The **Sunderbans** in the Ganga's delta is one of the world's largest **mangrove forests**. This World Heritage Site has crocodiles, hawksbill turtles, dolphins, river terrapins and man-eating tigers. Dakshinroy, the tiger-god, and Ma Bonobibi, a forest goddess, are worshipped here. Because tigers rarely attack when watched, honey-gatherers and fishermen wear masks behind their heads.

Duar means 'door', and the 8800-sq-km lowland Duar belt in northern Bengal and Assam links the plains with the Himalayas. Passes here form the entry or 'duar' into Bhutan. The region has grasslands, forests, tea plantations, sanctuaries and national parks. It is part of the Terai grassland belt.

Jaldapara WS, made up of tall Savannah type grasses, is in the Duars. It is a habitat for the endangered one-horned Indian rhinoceroses, different deer species, leopards, tigers, elephants, eight species of fresh water turtles; and birds like the Bengal florican, crested eagle and pied hornbill. Near the WS is a village where the Toto tribe lives.

Shantiniketan ashram was founded by Debendranath Tagore, Rabindranath's father, in 1863. Rabindranath established an experimental school here in 1901, which grew into the Visva Bharati University by 1921, with subjects as varied as fine arts, languages, technology and teacher training.

Darjeeling grew as a hill station after the monastery of Dorje Ling was spotted by a British officer in 1828. Set at 6982 ft, it once had fir and wild flower forests. It faces deforestation now. Four of the world's highest peaks, including Kanchenjunga (28,208 ft), are here. The Darjeeling Himalayan Railway, built in 1881, is a World Heritage Site.

Satyajit Ray, Ritwik Ghatak and Mrinal Sen directed some great films. Ray made *Pather Panchali* (based on Bibhutibhusan Bandopadhyay's 1928 novel) and ***Goopy Gyne Bagha Byne*** (based on Upendrakishore's story). Ghatak's films—like *Meghe Dhaka Tara*—influenced many young filmmakers. Mrinal Sen's *Bhuvan Shome* (1969) is considered a landmark in Indian cinema.

Arts & Crafts

Vishnupur in Bankura district is famous for its terracotta temples and its classical music. Its long-necked **Bankura horses** are a symbol for Indian handicrafts. Bamboo and stone tools are used to make them. Each part is made separately and then joined, smoothened, dried and baked.

Modern Indian art really began with the rough, bold and fresh **Kalighat** style of painting that grew around Kolkata's Kali temple from the mid-1900s to the 1920s. Initially, patua or scroll artists painted quick watercolours of deities on handmade paper. But soon funny scenes from everyday life were also painted.

Bengal's **woven textiles** are famous. Hand-woven Baluchari silk saris have designs from miniature paintings. The body of the Jamdani is woven from delicate muslin or cotton, while its geometric or floral designs are woven using coarser threads to give it a 'raised' look. A Jamdani sari takes months to weave.

Fact File

- **Date of formation**: January 26, 1950
  Size: 88,752 sq km
  Population: 80,176,197
  Capital: Kolkata
- **Rivers**: Hooghly, Teesta, Torsa, Subarnarekha, Joldhara
  Forests and NPs: Sunderbans Tiger Reserve, Jaldapara WS
- **Languages**: Bengali, Hindi, Urdu

Neighbours: **National**: Sikkim, Assam, Bihar, Jharkhand, Orissa
International: Bangladesh, Nepal, Bhutan
State Animal: Fishing cat
State Bird: White-throated kingfisher
State Tree: Devil tree or chatian
State Flower: Shephali

Orissa

Orissa was called Utkala, Kalinga and Odra Desa after the Okkala, Kalinga and Odra tribes who ruled it. Around the 1st century AD, Kalinga was a great sea-faring kingdom, and traded with Greece. The Greeks called the tribes Kalingai and Oretes. Later, Odra desa became 'Odissa', and under the British, came to be called 'Orissa'.

Ancient Buddhist texts refer to Kalinga around the time of the Buddha's death. Mahapadma Nanda conquered it around the 4th century BC. In the 3rd century BC, **Ashoka**, the Mauryan emperor, fought the battle of Kalinga to conquer it. Afterwards, he repented the bloodshed he had caused and converted to Buddhism.

Emperor Kharavela ruled Kalinga in the 1st century BC. The Bhauma Karas, Somavamshis, Gangas and Suryas followed. Afghans conquered it in 1568, and Emperor Akbar took over between 1590 and 1592. In the mid-1700s, the Bengal Nawabs and the Marathas ruled here, while the British took over in 1803.

Bhubaneshwar

Orissa has 62 tribes, like the Santhals, Savaras, Juangs, Gonds, **Bondas**, Oraons and Bhuinas. Like tribal societies elsewhere, they are known for their equality. Dormitories—like the Juang's Majang—taught young people life skills like art and dancing.

The spectacular Sun temple or **Surya Deul** of Konark was built by Narasimha I (1238-1264) of the Ganga dynasty. Shaped like a chariot, the massive, richly-carved temple has seven galloping horses which could symbolise the days of the week. The 24 intricately-worked wheels probably represent the hours of the day.

The **Jagannatha temple** of Puri was built by King Anantavarman Chodagangadeva (1078-1147) of the Ganga dynasty. During the annual Rath Yatra, idols of Krishna, Balabhadra and Subhadra are taken out in massive chariots called Nandighosa, Taladhwaja and Deviratha. The English word 'juggernaut' comes from the sight of these towering chariots.

The 33 sandstone caves on the **Udaygiri** and **Khandagiri** hills in Bhubaneshwar were probably carved under Kharavela. Though small, they have detailed inscriptions and carvings of royal processions and daily life. Udaygiri's double-storied Rani Gumpha and Khandagiri's Tatowa Gumpha or parrot cave are famous.

The only lake with partly salty water in India is coastal Orissa's endangered **Lake Chilika**, a Ramsar Site. The Chilika Lake Bird Sanctuary attracts the most migratory waterbird species in India every winter. It has 321 fish and crab species, a rare limbless lizard and the Irrawaddy dolphin.

Apart from a few other Indian beaches, **Olive Ridley turtles** come to the Gahirmatha, Devi and Rushikulya beaches in Orissa to lay their eggs. The turtles have olive green, heart-shaped shells and lay many eggs. But few hatchlings survive. Pollution, nets, bright industrial lights and the building of the Dhamra port near the beaches endanger their future.

Once known as Odra-Magadhi, **Odissi** dance originated in temples. Most Odissi performances are set to songs from the *Gitagovindam,* a Sanskrit poem written in the 12th century by Jayadeva. Tribhangi is a unique and complex Odissi movement, where the head, chest and pelvis move independently.

Bhitarkanika Sanctuary, near Gahirmatha, is set in India's second largest mangrove forest. This Ramsar Site protects giant salt-water crocodiles and 62 mangrove species. It is home to 215 species of birds, with eight kinds of kingfisher alone.

Simlipal NP, a part of Project Tiger, has around 1000 plant species, over 200 bird species, reptiles and large mammals. It has sal forests, grasslands, meadows, valleys, moist forests and dry deciduous ones. It takes its name from the semul or red silk-cotton tree.

Juangs perform the **Changu** dance, and bear and pigeon dances. Gadabas perform the Demsa during festivals, while Gonds dance regularly. Paraja girls dance holding a bunch of peacock feathers, accompanied by instruments like the dudunga.

Arts & Crafts

Chitrakars here paint intricate, bright and cheerful **pattachitras** on palm-leaf, ganjifa cards and cloth. Lampblack and crushed and boiled shells are used to make the colours.

Many tribes in Orissa like the Juangs, Dangaria Kandhs, Kutia Kandhs, Desia Kandhs, Duruas, Koyas and Lanjia Saoras craft **intricate combs** using bamboo, lac and fabric. They are prized and gifted as tokens of love.

The bright appliqué work of **Pipili** village is used in rituals, especially during the Rath Yatra. Pieces of cloth are cut, arranged and stitched on to larger fabric. Parrots, ducks, peacocks, elephants, crescents, the sun and Rahu are popular motifs.

Bomkai, Sambalpur and Sonepur are famous weaving villages. The smooth Sambalpuri **double ikat** has fish and conch-shell patterns. Some tribes still weave using wooden looms and bamboo fibre.

Fact File

Date of formation: August 15, 1947
Size: 1,55,707 sq km
Population: 36,804,660
Capital: Bhubaneshwar
Rivers: Mahanadi, Baitarni, Brahmani, Tel, Pushikulya, Sabari
Forests and NPs: Chilika Lake Sanctuary, Simlipal NP, Bhitarkanika WS

Language: Oriya
Neighbours: Andhra Pradesh, Chhattisgarh, Jharkhand, West Bengal
State Animal: Sambar
State Bird: Blue jay
State Tree: Ashwatha or peepal
State Flower: Ashoka

Sikkim

Sikkim is tucked away near India's tallest mountain range. It has enchanting monasteries and an amazing variety of flora and fauna. It is also home to beautiful crafts, masked dances and the endangered red panda.

Lepchas, Naongs, Changs and Mons were among the early settlers here. Bhutias came here from Tibet and Bhutan around the 14th century. British rule in Sikkim began in 1817.

Tiny, thumb-shaped Sikkim is known by different names. Lepchas call it **Nye-Mayel-Lyang** or 'heavenly hidden paradise'; Bhutias call it Denzong or 'the valley of rice'; and it was Beyul-Demojong or the 'hidden valley of rice and fruits' to Guru Rimpoche. 'Sikkim' could have come from the Limbu word 'su him' meaning 'new house'.

Gangtok

The Nyingmapa and Kagyupa sects of Buddhism are practised in Sikkim. But before that the older, animistic religion of **Bon** thrived here. Many Bon practices and beliefs were absorbed into Buddhism. Some Lepchas still follow Bon.

Nepalis came in much after the Bhutias, and brought with them cardamom and methods of terrace farming.

Limbus live in stone houses, at a height of 4000 ft above sea level. They grow their own food and keep domestic animals.

Sikkim has around 200 monasteries or Gompas where red-robed **lamas** chant to drums, horns and trumpets. Gompas have wall murals and frescos of Buddhist myths, manuscripts, thangkas and spinning prayer wheels. The pagoda-shaped Enchey monastery, built in 1909, is famous, as is Pemayangtse which was built in the 1600s.

Crowned in 1642, Chogyal Phuntsog Namgyal was Sikkim's first king. His dynasty ruled till 1975, when a large majority voted to merge with India. Chogyal **Palden Thondup Namgyal** was Sikkim's last king. The Namgyal Institute of Tibetology was started in 1958. It is in Gangtok and has rare books, thangkas, manuscripts and bronzes.

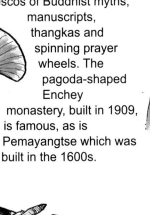

At 5800 ft above sea level, **Rumtek Gompa** houses the Kagyupa sect of Buddhism. Its leader Karmapa Rangjung Rigpe Dorje came here in 1959. Rumtek, an old Kagyupa monastery, was re-built as the Karmapa's home in exile.

The altitude in Sikkim varies dramatically from 300 m to 5000 m above sea level, leading to a rich biodiversity. It has **different ecological zones** which merge into one another: tropical, sub-tropical, temperate and alpine, and trans-Himalayan. Sal trees and orchids grow in the lower, sub-tropical zone; oaks, chestnuts and magnolias in the temperate; and junipers, cypresses and 35 rhododendron species in the alpine region. The trans-Himalayan region is a cold desert.

Though the **red panda** is said to live in six protected areas in Sikkim, in the wild it is highly endangered. The loss of its habitat, which happens when trees are cut, is the main reason for its disappearance. Road-building and over-grazing by cattle are other reasons.

The Khangchendzonga NP set up in 1977, has been declared a Biosphere Reserve. It ranges from 1829 m to 8550 m above sea level. Shy animals like the snow leopard, the **Himalayan tahr** and the yak live within this ecosystem.

Fambong La WS in the sub-tropical zone has oaks, bamboos, ferns, wild orchids and rhododendrons. Kyongnosla Alpine Sanctuary, 3292 m above sea level, has soaring silver firs, junipers and rare ground orchids. Musk deer and the endangered red panda roam here.

The world's third highest mountain (8586 m) is **Kanchenjunga** or Khangchendzonga as the Sikkimese call it. It is worshipped as Dzonga, the chief deity of Sikkim. Pang Lhabsol is celebrated to give it thanks. During the Chaam, Dzonga is represented as red-faced and riding the mythical snow lion.

On festivals, lamas or monks perform the Chaam, a masked dance, accompanied by the droning trumpet-like kangling, copper horns or radong, cymbals, gongs and drums. They wear richly-coloured robes and painted masks. A favourite character is Mahakala, the Great Protector. Jesters or **atchars** make people laugh.

Arts & Crafts

Thangkas or religious scroll paintings depict scenes from the Buddha's life, illustrate Buddhist beliefs or help people meditate. While drawing thangkas, artists have to stick to ancient rules of proportion and purity.

A **sand mandala** is made and destroyed as a symbol of the Buddhist belief that worldly things are not permanent. A group of monks creates an intricate, perfectly geometric design. They take weeks to fill it up with coloured sand. It is then wiped out ceremonially.

Bhutia women use wooden frame-looms and coloured wool to weave **hand-knotted carpets**. This method is the world's oldest form of carpet weaving. The dazzlingly colourful carpets have flowers, geometric designs, Buddhist figures, dragons and mythical birds known as dak and jira.

Fact File

Date of formation: May 16, 1975
Size: 7096 sq km
Population: 5,40,851
Capital: Gangtok
Rivers: Teesta, Rangit
Forests and NPs: Khangchendzonga NP and Fambong La WS
Languages: Lepcha, Bhutia, Limbu, Nepali, Hindi

Neighbours: National: West Bengal
International: China, Nepal, Bhutan
State Animal: Red panda
State Bird: Blood pheasant
State Tree: Nobile orchid
State Flower: Rhododendron

Asom

Asom used to be known as **Assam.** Most Northeastern states were once part of this state and were carved out after independence. Asom has forests, hills and is a rich source of oil, gas and tea. It is also home to the one-horned rhinoceros and Majuli, a large river island.

The ancient kingdom of **Kamarupa**, as Asom was known, stretched to Bhutan, Bangladesh and Cooch Behar in West Bengal. Many dynasties ruled here, like the Pala, Koch, Kachari and Chutiya. But the Ahoms who came from Myanmar were the strongest. After repeated attacks by Myanmar, the British signed the Treaty of Yandabo with them in 1826, making Assam a part of the British empire in India.

Asom has three main **geographical regions:** the Brahmaputra valley to the north, the Karbi Anglong and North Cachar Hills in between, and the Barak valley to the south.

Dispur

Though Dispur is its capital, Guwahati is one of Asom's most important cities. It was the capital of the Kamrupa kingdom and was called Pragjyotishpur or the 'city of eastern astrology'. It has a **Navagraha temple** devoted to the nine planets.

Hajo, on the northern bank of the Brahmaputra, is a centre of pilgrimage for Muslims, Buddhists and Hindus. The Hayagriva-Madhab temple in the village draws Buddhists and Hindus, while Muslims pray at Poa-Mecca, which was built by Pir Giasuddin Aulia. It is called 'poa' or 'one-fourth' because it is believed to have a quarter of the sanctity of Mecca.

Nameri NP near the Arunachal border has elephants, sloth bears and Indian soft-shelled turtles. The rare atlas moth which has a wing-span of 10 inches has been spotted here.

Manas NP, in the Himalayan foothills, is a World Heritage Site and a tiger sanctuary. Its other rare inmates are the hispid hare, **pigmy hog**, golden langur and the rhinoceros.

Tezpur, a tea centre, is in Sonitpur district. It was called the 'city of blood' after a mythical battle between Shiva and Vishnu filled it with blood. It has a 9th century temple complex in the Bamuni Hills.

Majuli Island, on the River Brahmaputra, is one of the world's largest river islands. Some parts are inhabited by tribes like the Mishing, the Deoris and the Sonowal Kachari. The 880-sq-km island is becoming smaller because of erosion by the Brahmaputra.

Kaziranga NP is home to the famous **one-horned rhinoceros.** It is the oldest NP in Asom and is a World Heritage Site. It has forests, elephant grass and marshes. Apart from other animals, it has hog badgers, capped langurs and the subcontinent's only **ape**, the hoolock gibbon.

The **Ahom** dynasty ruled here for nearly 600 years. In Bhomoraguri, a huge stone inscription says that the Ahom general Kalia Bhomora Phukan had planned to construct a bridge across the Brahmaputra. About 200 years later, a bridge was built at the spot and named after him.

Asom has large reserves of **oil, natural gas and coal**. Oil was discovered in Digboi in the late 1800s. The first oil well in India was drilled here in 1889, and the first modern refinery started production in 1901.

Asom produces **half of India's tea** and about one-sixth of the world's. Robert Bruce, a British officer, learned about tea grown by the Singpho tribe in Asom in 1823. He befriended the chief, Bessa Gam, and was gifted plants and seeds. He felt that Asom tea could one day bring in as much revenue for the British as China tea.

Asom makes three unique silks—the golden Muga, the white Pat and the warm Eri. The entire village of **Sualkuchi** near Guwahati is involved with weaving Muga silks. Silks grown everywhere in Asom find their way here. Muga is special because it actually glows more after each wash.

Every community here has its own distinctive design and style of weaving. Borders have stylised creepers, animals, people, flowers and even stars. Traditional garments like the **mekhela-chador** and the gamosa (towel) have beautiful borders.

Arts & Crafts

Sankaradeva, a 15th century saint-poet, was part of the Bhakti movement. He set up **satras** or monasteries that would also preserve art and culture. There are around 20 satras in Majuli, each devoted to a different art form, ranging from jewellery to mask-making. He created a form of classical dance called Sattriya Nrittya.

Toys in Asom were traditionally made of clay, pith (or cork), wood, bamboo, cloth and a combination of cloth-and-mud. Each kind of material is used to make a different type of toy. Birds, animals, gods, and brides and grooms are the most popular figures.

Cane and bamboo were once used to make everything from houses to musical instruments, sieves, baskets and hats. The **Jappi** is the traditional hat or sunshade made out of bamboo. It is used by people working in the fields.

Fact File

Date of formation: January 26, 1950
Size: 78,438 sq km
Population: 26,655,528
Capital: Dispur
Rivers: Brahmaputra, Manas, Subansiri, Sonai
Forests and NPs: Kaziranga NP, Manas NP, Orang Sanctuary
Languages: Assamese, Bodo, Karbi, Bengali

Neighbours: National: Meghalaya, Arunachal Pradesh, Nagaland, Manipur, Tripura, Mizoram, West Bengal; **International:** Bhutan, Bangladesh
State Animal: One-horned rhinoceros
State Bird: White winged wood duck
State Flower: Foxtail orchid
State Tree: Hollong

Arunachal Pradesh

Arunachal Pradesh (AP) is a lush green state, which is still around 80% forest. It has different kinds of forests: tropical, subtropical, pine, temperate and alpine. Bamboo forests, degraded forests and grasslands are also found here. Most of the forests are evergreen—so they stay green and leafy all year round.

The Brahmaputra is known as the **Siang** in AP. The Siang and its tributaries divide AP into five river valleys: the Kameng, the Subansiri, the Siang, the Lohit and the Tirap. The tributaries have rivulets large and small, which get their waters from snow melted off the Himalayas.

Itanagar

AP has about 26 major tribes which are divided by geography, religion and cultural practices. The Monpas, Sherdukpens and many others are Buddhists; the Adis, Akas, **Apatanis** and others worship the Sun and the Moon Gods; while the Wanchos and Noctes live in Tirap, near Nagaland. Noctes worship Vishnu.

The Dihang Dibang Biosphere Reserve is a global biodiversity hotspot. Apart from this, AP has eight WSs and two NPs. Its forests have three kinds of leopards, seven kinds of **primates** (for example, macaques, gibbons and langurs), three types of goat-antelopes, and birds like Temminck's tragopan and the **white-winged duck**.

In AP, **climate** varies with elevation or height. In the Himalayas, it is cold and alpine, while a little lower, the climate is temperate. Parts of AP that are closer to the sea, are subtropical and hot. Every year, AP gets about 3500 mm of rain.

The first people to live in Arunachal Pradesh were probably of Tibetan and Myanmari descent. AP became a part of British India in 1826. Once known as the **North East Frontier Agency**, it became a union territory in 1972, and was called Arunachal Pradesh. It became a state in 1987. China disputes the 890-km-long northern boundary of the state, called the McMahon Line.

Festivals like **Losar**, Si-Donyi and Reh, among others, are closely linked to the phases of farming. All year round, one tribe or the other celebrates a festival. Spring, for example, is celebrated between January and April by different tribes. Festivals draw together tribe members who live far away.

Adis and Apatanis used to follow shifting cultivation or jhum, which has now been discontinued. Adis have split-level granaries made of bamboo which are cleverly built to keep away rats. The **Idu** tribe is divided into clans, each named after the river which flows by the place where they live.

Because it ranges between 200 m to 4500 m, **Namdapha NP** has a variety of climate types and perhaps the widest diversity of habitats among South Asia's protected areas. Unusually, it has four large cats—tigers, leopards, clouded leopards and snow leopards—within its limits.

Dances are a part of most festivals, and each tribe has its own dance—like the Chalo dance (Noctes), the **Lion and Peacock dance** (Monpas), Ponung (Adis), and the Roppi (Nishing). Most dances are performed by both men and women.

AP has around 600 rare species of orchids like the **foxtail orchid**. The town of Tipi has an Orchid Research and Development Station. Sessa has a large Orchid Sanctuary as well.

Monpas, who are Buddhists, live in the mountains of western AP. The famous **Tawang Gompa** here is the second largest Buddhist monastery in Asia. Built like a walled city, it has homes for the monks, a library and a museum. Some of its buildings are nearly 350 years old.

Cattle known as **mithun** are an important part of the social, religious and cultural life of many tribes. The mithun is considered a unit of wealth and is allowed to roam free till it is sacrificed and eaten on special occasions.

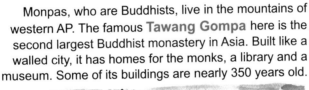

Arts & Crafts

Objects of everyday use are often made out of cane, bamboo, **wood** and fabric. Monpas are especially good woodcarvers and make ceremonial masks, cups and dishes out of wood. They make paper from the pulp of the Sukso or the paper tree.

Women in AP are expert **weavers**, with a great sense of colour and design. They use black, yellow, blue, green and red in their geometric weaves. Idu-Mishmi women weave different kinds of diamond patterns into their fabrics.

Bamboo, beads, feathers and wings of insects like green beetles are used to make necklaces and other ornaments here. Some tribes use **hornbill beaks** to decorate their tightly-wound cane helmets. Of late, real beaks are replaced by artificial ones.

Fact File

- **Date of formation**: February 20, 1987
- **Size**: 83,743 sq km
- **Population**: 10,97,968
- **Capital**: Itanagar
- **Rivers**: Siang and its tributaries: Lohit, Kameg, Dikrong, Tirap, Dibang, Subansiri, Noa-Dihing, Kamlang
- **Forests and NPs**: Namdapha NP, Monling NP

- **Languages**: Monpa, Miji, Aka, Sherdukpen, Apatani, Adi, Hill Miri
- **Neighbours**: **National**: Assam, Nagaland; **International**: China, Bhutan, Myanmar
- **State bird**: Great Indian hornbill
- **State animal**: Mithun
- **State flower**: Foxtail orchid

Nagaland

is hilly, rugged and beautiful. The Aos, a Naga tribe, believe that a magician called Changkichanglangba had told his people that a surprise awaited them if they opened his grave on the sixth day after he died. The people found basketry designs there and copied them to create many useful, ingenious and delightful objects.

Ahom records of the many Naga tribes tell us about Nagaland's history and practices. In 1819 it was conquered by **Myanmar** and came under British rule in 1826. After 1947, many Naga tribes demanded that they be allowed to break away from India.

Geologically, the hills of Nagaland are a part of the Burma group. They join the sub-Himalayan ranges in the north and stretch as far as Manipur. There are tall mountains, bottomless gorges and lush valleys full of amazing natural life. **Saramati**, 3826 m above sea level, is Nagaland's highest peak; Japfu, at 3048 m, is the second highest.

Kohima

Dimapur has an elaborately-carved gateway, Kachari ruins and **monolithic sites**. It used to be the capital of the ancient Kachari kings and was once known as Hidimbapur. Bhima, the Pandava, is supposed to have married a Kachari princess called Hidimba. The River Dimasa flows here.

Naga languages belong to the **Tibeto-Burman** language group. Each tribe is distinct, with its own dialect, cultural practices and beliefs, and methods of weaving baskets and shawls.

Naga festivals—Moatsu, Nazu, Tuluni, and many more—are tied to the farming year. The Ao **Tsüngrem Mong** is celebrated just before harvest.

The **Angami** festival of Sekrenyi is celebrated after harvest. Young men wear new white shawls called Mhoushus and black ones called Lohe. Among the rituals are Thekra chi, when young people gather together to sing songs and drink rice beer. The interesting ritual of gate-pulling takes place on the eighth day.

Of the 20 Naga tribes and sub-tribes, the **Konyak**, Ao, Chang, Phom and Lotha live in Nagaland, while others like the Nocte and Wancho live in neighbouring Arunachal Pradesh. With changing times, their rich cultural practices and beliefs are slowly dying out.

Nagaland's capital, **Kohima**, is 1444 m above sea-level. The Catholic Cathedral at Aradurah Hill is the largest in the Northeast. Kohima probably grew from an Angami village called Barra Basti, now believed to be the second largest village in Asia. Like many other Naga villages, it has an elaborately carved wooden gate.

Malabar pied hornbills, blue rock pigeons, spotted doves, hoopoes, common babblers, great horned owls and spotted owlets make up the many **bird species** here. The rarer species are white-bellied herons, Blyth's tragopans, Mrs Hume's bartailed pheasants, brown-backed hornbills, rufous-necked hornbills, wreathed hornbills and green peafowls.

. . . .

Reptiles and different species of turtles are endangered by poaching and **habitat loss** caused by the cutting down of forests. Poaching and habitat loss also threaten tigers, binturongs, leopards and clouded leopards. The four WSs here—Intanki, Fakim, Pulie Badge and Rangapahar—are small.

. . . .

The most common species of orchid in Nagaland is the **dendrobium**. The bamboo orchid, red vanda, red chimney orchid and foxtail orchid are the rare ones. While Mount Japfu has the most number of orchids, Tuensang district has the most threatened and rare species.

Forests here have elephants, primates, northern tree shrews, wild dogs or dholes, sun bears, **binturongs** and Malayan tree squirrels. Binturongs belong to the civet family, though they are sometimes called 'bearcats'. Their long, bushy tails are prehensile—they can be used to hold on to things by curling around them.

. . . .

An amazing **360 orchid species** are found on peaks like Saramati and in low-lying areas. They are adaptable, and manage to grow in soil (terrestrials), on trees (epiphytes), on rocks and in thin soil (lithophytes), and on decaying matter (saprophytes). The smallest are 1 cm to 2 cm, and the largest are more than 2 m.

. . . .

Nagas share a close relationship with **bamboo groves** because each species of bamboo has a different use for them. Houses, utensils, torches, fuel, pickles, mats, furniture, pokerwork mugs, pipes, hats, shields and cradles are all made with bamboo.

Some tribes weave necklaces and arm bands using red-coloured **cane** strips, yellow orchid stems and shells. Rain hats, bowls, mugs, coarse baskets and even haversacks made of cane are common.

Arts & Crafts

Naga baskets are usually of two kinds: baskets for storage and baskets for carrying. Some are woven so tightly, they can even hold liquids. Aos weave **conical baskets**, while Angamis prefer cylindrical ones. The Chakhesangs, Angami Nagas and Changs also weave baskets in different designs.

Aos use a hard kind of bamboo and a gourd to make the **cup violin** or the midnight violin. It has a thin, long bamboo bow. Its strings are made of bamboo fibre cut using a dao or sharp axe. Aos say they learned to play it by watching the way a crab moves!

The **bamboo trumpet**, considered the king of musical instruments, is made out of a bamboo shoot which is about 4 ft to 5 ft long. At six inches, the bamboo mouth organ is much smaller. It is one of the oldest Naga musical instruments.

Fact File

Date of formation: December 1,1963
Size: 16,579 sq km
Population: 19,88,636
Capital: Kohima
Rivers: Milak, Barak, Dhansiri, Doyang, Dikhu, Zungki, Tizu
Forests and NPs: Intanki NP
Languages: Ao, Sema, Konyak, Angami, Chakhesang, Chang, Khiamniungan, Kuki

Neighbours: National: Arunachal Pradesh, Assam, Manipur
International: Myanmar
State Animal: Mithun
State Bird: Blyth's tragopan
State Tree: Alder
State Flower: Rhododendron

Meghalaya

or 'the abode of clouds' has many unique tribes, forests, animals and art forms. It is also the home of a tiny carnivorous plant called the 'basket of the devil', a butterfly called the Bhutan glory, and a fruit called the 'orange of the spirits'.

The Jaintias, Khasis, Garos, Koch, Hajong, Dimasa, Hmar, Kuki, Lakhar, Mikir, Rabha and other tribes live here. Garos call themseves Achik-Mande or 'hill people'. Khasis, Jaintias, Bhois and Wars are together known as the Hynniew Trep people.

Khasis and Jaintias follow the matrilineal system. This means that women inherit land, social rank and name. The youngest daughter or the 'Ka Khadduh' inherits the family's fortunes. Khasis live in the eastern part of Meghalaya.

We know about Meghalaya's early history from Ahom and Kachari records of Khasi kings. The British ruled here from the 1830s. Though Meghalaya was a part of Assam after 1947, Jawaharlal Nehru ensured that its tribal traditions and practices were protected.

Shillong

The Lum Sohpetbneng peak has a sacred forest. Khasis call it 'heavenly peak' and believe that it used to be a golden staircase between earth and heaven. Sixteen families used to go up and down. Seven chose to stay back and were called the Hynniew Trep.

Garos celebrate a good harvest with Wangala, or the Dance of Hundred Drums in November. People dress in feathered head-dresses and dance to the beat of long drums in honour of Satyong, the god of fertility.

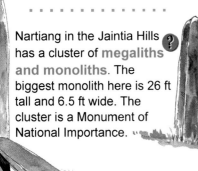

Nartiang in the Jaintia Hills has a cluster of megaliths and monoliths. The biggest monolith here is 26 ft tall and 6.5 ft wide. The cluster is a Monument of National Importance.

Meghalaya's many stunning cave systems like Krem Liatprah (25 km), Umlawan, Mawsynram and Siju, among others, are long and deep. Most have huge limestone formations inside. Krem Liatprah is in danger because of the limestone and coal mining operations nearby.

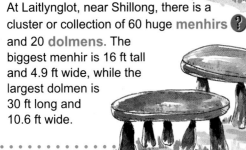

At Laitlynglot, near Shillong, there is a cluster or collection of 60 huge menhirs and 20 dolmens. The biggest menhir is 16 ft tall and 4.9 ft wide, while the largest dolmen is 30 ft long and 10.6 ft wide.

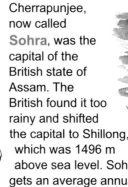

Cherrapunjee, now called Sohra, was the capital of the British state of Assam. The British found it too rainy and shifted the capital to Shillong, which was 1496 m above sea level. Sohra gets an average annual rainfall of 11,430 mm.

Laitkynsew village near Sohra has sturdy **living root bridges**. Khasi tribes built them by stretching the secondary roots of a single rubber tree and planting them on the other side of a stream or river. A living root bridge in Nongriat village has two levels—almost as if one bridge had been placed on the other.

The rare **pitcher plant** is called memang-koksi or the 'basket of the devil' by the Garos. It has a small leaf that looks and acts like a lid and traps insects, which it then 'eats'. It is protected in the Baghmara Pitcher Plant Sanctuary.

About **300 orchid species** grow here, on trees, the ground and mossy rocks. Mawsmai and Mawmluh forests in Sohra have the most. Forests and everything in them were once considered sacred by tribes and protected. Nowadays, orchids are protected in orchidaria and orchid sanctuaries.

The blue peacock, karserhed, orange oak leaf, dipper and **Bhutan glory** are all names of Meghalaya's beautiful and famous butterfly species.

Nongkhyllem WS in Ri Bhoi is part of the Eastern Himalayan Endemic Bird Area. It has endangered bird species like the swamp partridge, brown hornbill, rufous-necked hornbill and the **Manipur bush quail**

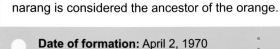

Balpakram NP has hoolock gibbons, great Indian hornbills, tigers and leopards. Called 'the land of eternal wind', it is sacred to the Garos because they believe that dead spirits rest here. Ground orchids and a citrus fruit called me-mang narang or 'the orange of the spirits' grow here. The narang is considered the ancestor of the orange.

Nokrek NP and Biosphere Reserve is on Nokrek, the highest peak in the Garo Hills. It has villages, rare plants, wild elephants and rare birds as well. Me-mang narang trees grow here.

Fact File

Date of formation: April 2, 1970
Size: 22,429 sq km
Population: 23,18,822
Capital: Shillong
Rivers: Simsang, Manda, Darming, Ringge, Gamol, Bugi,
Forests and NPs: Nokrek NP, Balpakram NP, Nongkhyllem WS, Nokrek Biosphere Reserve, Siju Bird Sanctuary

Languages: Khasi, Garo, Jaintia, Bengali, Assamese, English
Neighbours: National: Assam
International: Bangladesh
State Animal: Clouded leopard
State Bird: Hill myna
State Tree: Gamhar
State Flower: Lady slipper orchid

Arts & Crafts

Traditionally, only women used to spin and **weave** here. They would weave only after the harvest of new rice was eaten. Khasis and Garos make colourful wraps, shawls, waistcloths, scarves, skirts, aprons and lungis. Meghalaya is also famous for its Endi silk.

Khasis and Garos weave cane baskets and sieves. Baskets called khok and thugis are common, but the Garos also weave more intricate ones called meghum khoks to hold clothes and valuables. The Khasis weave a cone-shaped bamboo rain-shield called **knup**.

Manipur

or the 'jewelled land' is like a bright green emerald surrounded by mountain ranges. The state has two parts—the outer hilly area and the inner Manipur River valley. Much of Manipur is still heavily forested, making it a treasure-house of rare orchids, birds and animals.

Manipur's earliest recorded history goes as far back as AD 900. Following constant attacks from Myanmar, **Raja Jai Singh** signed a treaty with the British in 1762. They took over the kingdom after 1891.

Imphal

The 312-sq-km Lake Loktak near Imphal, is the largest lake in eastern India and has small floating masses of vegetation called **phumdis**. The lake is a source of livelihood for the many

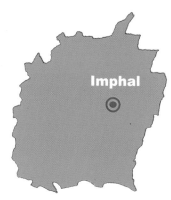

people who live on and around it. This Ramsar Site also protects the people who live near it from floods and droughts.

Manipur has 29 or more tribes, like the **Meitei**, Naga, Kuki, Meitei Pangal and others. The tribes' cultural practices, beliefs, folklore, dances, games, martial arts, music, weaving styles and crafts are different from each other.

The **Keibul Lamjao NP** is set on a large phumdi on Lake Loktak, and is the only floating NP in the world. It stretches over 40 sq km. It has otters, water birds and migratory birds.

Keibul Lamjao also has the endangered **sangai**, or the Manipur brow-antlered deer. Sangai live in small herds and hide during the day. They are also called 'dancing deer' because of their delicate walk through the wetlands.

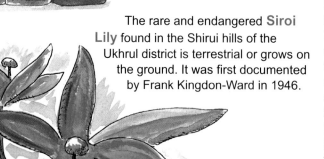

Imphal has an all-women's market or **Ima keithel**. The stalls are run by 3000 Imas or mothers. The market has two parts: vegetables, fruits, fish and groceries are sold in one, and exquisite handlooms and household tools are sold in the other.

The rare and endangered **Siroi Lily** found in the Shirui hills of the Ukhrul district is terrestrial or grows on the ground. It was first documented by Frank Kingdon-Ward in 1946.

The **Samban-Lei Sekpil**, grown by Moirangthem Okendra Kumbi, is a 61-ft-tall topiary or shaped shrub. It is so tall that you need a ladder to reach the top. Trimmed into umbrella and disc shapes, it holds the Guinness and the Limca records for being the tallest topiary in the world.

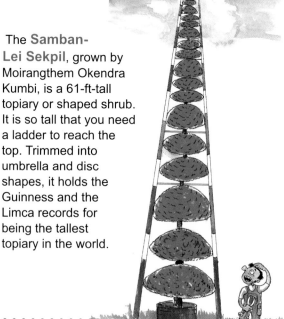

Manipur has a variety of animal and bird species like hoolock gibbon, slow loris, **clouded leopard**, spotted linshang, Mrs Hume's barbacked pheasant, Blyth's tragopan, and the Burmese pea-fowl. Its **hornbill** species are: the brown-backed, the rufous-necked, the wreathed, the Indian pied or the lesser pied and the great Indian hornbill.

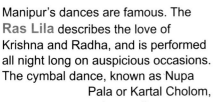

During the festival of Lai Haraoba, Meiteis have a dance in which their priestesses or **Maibis** re-live the past, starting with the process of creation, the construction of houses and the growth of different occupations.

The **Khonghampat Orchidarium** near Imphal in Manipur has about 110 rare orchids. These beautiful and rare plants are endangered because of deforestation and trade in orchids.

Manipur's dances are famous. The **Ras Lila** describes the love of Krishna and Radha, and is performed all night long on auspicious occasions. The cymbal dance, known as Nupa Pala or Kartal Cholom, is usually performed before the Ras Lila.

The **Pung** is the Manipuri version of the Mridanga, an ancient drum. It is played during the Ras Lila. It is also important enough to be worshipped through a dance called the Pung Cholom. The dancers leap as they play the Pung. Drumbeats vary from soft to thunderous.

Arts & Crafts

Fish traps in Manipur vary with regions, tribes and even genders. Women from the valley use bowl-shaped fishing baskets called Long, while their men use the Long-oop. Hill people use Kaijara fish-baskets and people living near Lake Loktak use the Ngathok.

Bamboo is used to make many things of daily use like **baskets**, fish traps, mats, roofs, cooking huts, granaries, musical instruments, headgear, umbrellas, totem poles and even small bridges. Bamboo musical instruments differ from tribe to tribe.

Fact File

Date of formation: January 21, 1972
Size: 22,327 sq km
Population: 22,93,896
Capital: Imphal
Rivers: Manipur, Barak
Forests and Nps: Keibul Lamjao NP, Khonghampat Orchidarium
Languages: Manipuri, Thado, Tangkhul

Neighbours: National: Assam, Mizoram, Nagaland
International: Myanmar
State Animal: Sangai deer
State Bird: Nongyeen
State Flower: Siroi lily

Mizoram

Mizoram or 'the land of the hill people' has 21 hill ranges. Nestled between Bangladesh and Myanmar, it has a 722-km-long international boundary. Many Mizos live by the codes of Tlawmngaihna and Hnatlang which tell them to be kind, hospitable, cooperative and helpful.

Phawngpui NP lies close to the Myanmar border. Mizoram's tallest peak, the Phawngpui or Blue Mountain, is inside the park and stands 2360 m above sea level. The park has gorals, serows, stump-tail macaques, langurs, barking deer and leopards.

The first Mizo tribes probably migrated to India from Shinlung or Chhinlungsan in China via Myanmar. The first to come here were the **Kukis**, and the last to do so in the late 1700s were the Lushais.

When the British took over nearby Assam in 1826, many Mizo chiefs attacked their territories. From 1890, when the British began to rule here, to 1972, Mizoram was a part of Assam. It became a state after much agitation under the **Mizoram Peace Accord** in 1987.

Aizawl

Mizoram's capital, **Aizawl**, lies just north of the Tropic of Cancer. The city is a little over 100 years old and is built like a fortress. It has timber houses and stands about 2950 ft above sea level, with river valleys to its east and west.

Most Mizos still farm the land. Their festivals like Mim, Pawl and Chapchar Kuts are linked to the farming year. Chapchar Kut celebrates spring, while **Mim Kut** gives thanks for a good harvest of maize. There is much singing, dancing and drinking of zu, the home-brewed rice beer. Pawl Kut, also a harvest festival, is celebrated during December and January.

Mizoram has many lakes like Palak, Tamdil, Rungdil and Rengdil. **Tamdil** or the 'lake of the mustard plant' is so called because according to Mizo legend a gigantic mustard plant once grew there. When it was chopped off, water spurted out, creating the lake.

The main social unit of Mizo life was the village, usually set on a hill-top with the chief's house in the middle. Young Mizo men lived in a large dormitory called the **Zawlbuk**, where they were trained to be responsible adults.

At 25 m, **Pukzing cave** near Aizawl, is the largest of the many caves in Mizoram. Legends say that Mualzavata, a very strong man, carved it out with a hair pin.

Mizo folk stories tell us that they first came out from under a huge rock called Chhinlung. Pathian (the Mizo word for god) was annoyed by the loud voices of two very talkative people. Fed up of their noisy chatter, he shut off the entrance with a rock.

Cheraw or the bamboo dance is colourful and popular. Men sit on the ground and rhythmically tap long pairs of bamboo sticks open and shut, while women dance in and out of them. Many Indonesian, Philippine and Thai tribes have similar dances, suggesting that the Cheraw probably came with Mizos from Southeast Asia.

The hoolock gibbon is the only ape found in the Indian subcontinent. It lives on trees, eats fruits, mates for life and lives in small family units. Hoolocks protect their territory and scare enemies with loud hooting noises. Sometimes mates 'sing' together as they swing across the forest.

Lengteng WS's height ranges between 400 m and 2300 m above sea level. It has the second highest peak of Mizoram and animals like tigers, sambars, serows, gorals, barking deer, wild boars, hoolock gibbons and rhesus macaques; apart from birds like the Hume's bartailed pheasant and the kaleej pheasant. Thorangtlang WS in the west is a corridor for elephants migrating from Bangladesh.

Arts & Crafts

Mizo men and women wore the **puan**, which was traditionally woven by women. The puan's woven designs and colours are distinctive and bright. Some of these designs are now an integral part of the Mizo heritage.

Using cane and bamboo, Mizos make an amazing range of beautiful, sturdy baskets, pipes, weapons and rain wear. Their traps cleverly use the **natural elasticity of bamboo** to spring shut when the prey touches it. They also use this elasticity to make toys like pop guns.

Some fish traps are bottle-shaped with a spike at the mouth, which stops the fish from escaping. **Fishing baskets** are oval or square in shape, and come with or without lids. They are used for tasks like trapping fish and carrying it.

Fact File

- **Date of formation:** February 20, 1987
  Size: 21,081 sq km
  Population: 8,91,058
  Capital: Aizawl
- **Rivers**: Tlwang, Tlau, Chhimtuipui, Tuichang, Tuirial
  Forests and NPs: Lengteng WS, Murlen NP, Phawngpui NP, Thorangtlang WS

Languages: Lushai, Mizo, Bengali, Lakher
Neighbours: **National**: Manipur, Assam, Tripura; **International**: Bangladesh, Myanmar
State Animal: Serow
State Bird: Hume's bartailed pheasant
State Tree: Nag kesar
State Flower: Dancing girl orchid

Tripura

Tripura is one of the smallest states in India and juts into Bangladesh like a finger. Tripurans have many unique games like matham, where children jump into a pond and behave like otters! Of the state's 19 tribes, the Tripuri tribe is the largest in number. Tripuris call themselves Borok, and speak Kok-borok or 'the language of people'.

From the mid-1400s, Tripura was ruled by kings who held the title of 'Manikya'. Tripura came under Mughal rule from the 1600s, and the British took over in the late 1700s. Tripura's capital was Udaipur, till Maharaja Krishna Kishore Manikya shifted it to new Agartala in 1849. King **Bir Chandra Manikya Bahadur Debbarma** introduced many reforms when he came to the throne in 1862.

Different tribes like the Halams, Jamatias, Reangs, Noatias, Mogs, Mundas and Lushais live here. **Nature deities** like Khuluma, the goddess of the cotton plant; Mailuma, the goddess of corn; Lam-Pra, the twin gods of the sky and the sea; and Burha-cha, the god of healing are worshipped here.

⊙ **Agartala**

The word 'Tripura' could have come from the name of the powerful King Tripur, or from the state's main goddess, Tripura Sundari. Some historians believe that 'Tripura' comes from two Kok-borok words: 'twi' or water, and 'pra' or near.

Udaipur is known for its many ancient temples and its large ponds or dighis. The most famous is the **Tripura Sundari temple** built by Maharaja Dhanya Manikya Debbarma in 1501. It is one of the 51 Shakti temples in the Indian subcontinent. It was built on a hillock and has a square-shaped sanctum.

The town of **Pilak** has terracotta, bronze, and rock-cut sculptures which were made between the 8th and the 10th centuries. They have a mix of Buddhist and Hindu themes, with influences ranging from the Bengali to the Myanmarese. They are scattered over an area of 10 sq km.

According to Tripuran folklore, the earth rests on **Kaiching**, a tortoise who feeds on human excreta brought to it by Khebok, a black beetle. Once, to avoid work, Khebok told Kaiching that the humans had all died. Kaiching shook his shell, causing an earthquake. When the people cried out, Kaiching hit Khebok on the head with a stone, leaving him flat-headed forever!

Lake Rudrsagar is the only lake in eastern India with a palace on it. **Neermahal** was built by Maharaja Bir Bikram Kishore Manikya Bahadur as a summer resort in 1930. Its domes are a blend of Hindu and Mughal styles. Rudrasagar is home to many migratory birds.

Sports are called **Thwngmung** as a group. Games like Swkwi, Fan Solaimung and Kaldong are a test of strength, skill and alertness. In Wah Sotonmung, a one-metre-long bamboo pole is held by two groups. Both pull at it, till one wins by pulling the other for more than one metre.

The Gumti WS draws many water birds to its large reservoir. Apart from barking deer, bisons, elephants, and wild goats, Gumti has medicinal plants. Trishna WS has wild cats, leopards, **spectacled langurs**, capped langurs, golden langurs and the hoolock gibbon.

Unakoti, meaning one-less-than-a-crore, is a collection of hundreds of bas-relief sculptures, stone carvings, temple ruins and sandstone sculptures on the banks of River Gomti. Unakotiswara Kal Bhairava is a 30-ft-high head of Shiva. Work on the sculptures probably went on from the 7th to the 9th centuries AD.

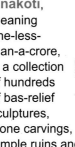

In Sepahijala WS, civets, barking deer and clouded leopards roam among the sal, agar, amlaki and bamboo trees. Primates like the capped langur, the spectacled langur and the pigtailed macaque live here. The **green imperial pigeon**, white ibis, and whistling teal are among its bird species.

Chakmas perform the Bijhu dance, while Reangs perform **Hojagiri**, a graceful dance done on pots. In the Lebang Boomani dance women chase insects called lebangs, which arrive in hoards to eat the freshly-sown seeds. Men use bamboo chips as clappers to make a noise which will draw out the lebangs.

In Tripura, singers are accompanied by instruments like the **sarinda**, chongpreng, dangdoo, lebang, kham, uakhrap and the bamboo flute or sumui.

Arts & Crafts

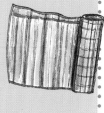

Thin bamboo splits are sometimes woven with cotton to make **mats** which are almost as pliable as fabric. Coloured yarn and dyed bamboo splits make them attractive.

Kuki women used to weave clothes with **snakeskin designs** on them called Ponmongvom, Khamtang and Saipi-khup. No one was allowed to cross water bodies wearing these fabrics, for fear that the designs would attract snakes.

Tripuri women use the loin-loom to weave garments called the **risa** and the **rignai**. The Lasingphee is made into a quilt at the time of weaving itself with the help of a thin lining of cotton.

Because bamboo is strong enough to **resist earthquakes** and strong winds, it is also used for making granaries, shops and houses here. Bamboo splits are made into screens and partitions. Finely-cut splits that look like ivory are used to make jewellery.

Fact File

Date of formation: January 21, 1972
Size: 10,491 sq km
Population: 31,99,203
Capital: Agartala
River: Gomti
Forests and NPs: Shepahijala WS, Trishna WS, Rowa WS
Languages: Kok-borok, Bengali, Manipuri

Neighbours: National: Arunachal Pradesh, Assam, Manipur
International: Myanmar
State Animal: Phayre's langur or spectacled langur
State Bird: Green imperial pigeon
State Tree: Agar
State Flower: Nageshwar

Madhya Pradesh

Madhya Pradesh stretches across central India. It has wildlife sanctuaries, cave paintings and ancient Stupas. But its greatest treasures are its dense forests which inspired everyone from prehistoric artists to the author Rudyard Kipling!

After the Maurya rule, the **Sungas** ruled MP from 185 BC to 73 BC. They were followed by the Satavahanas, Kshatrapas, Nagas, Guptas, Hunas, Kalachuris, Tomars and Gonds. In 1231 Sultan Shamsuddin Iltutmish took over, followed by the Khaljis and the Mughals. By the 1760s, different Maratha clans ruled here. In 1818, the British defeated them and took over.

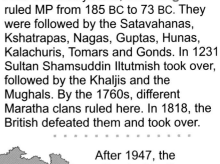

Bhopal

Rudyard Kipling's *The Jungle Book* has stories set in the forests of the Seoni district. One of them is about **Mowgli**, a boy raised by wolves. It was probably inspired by Sir William Sleeman's description of a wolf-boy found in 1831 near the Pench forest.

After 1947, the **Central India Agency** was divided into Madhya Bharat, Vindhya Pradesh and Bhopal. Later the Central Provinces and Berar were named 'Madhya Pradesh'. In 1956, Madhya Bharat, Vindhya Pradesh and Bhopal were merged with Madhya Pradesh.

MP's sprawling mountain ranges—the Vindhyas and Satpuras—have always been thought of as a **natural line** that divides India into north and south. The River Narmada flows in the valley of the two ranges.

Of the 700 or so rock shelters in **Bhimbetka**, 400 have prehistoric paintings done with natural red and white colours. The 10,000-year-old shelters were discovered by Prof. Wakankar in 1957. Animals like tigers, lions, wild boars, antelopes, dogs, lizards and crocodiles; and activities like hunting, dancing, playing music, collecting honey, decorating bodies and making masks are all depicted. It is a World Heritage Site.

OFFICIAL TIGER FIGURES

KANHA: 138
PENCH: 50
BANDHAVGARH: 50

Pench and Kanha forests in the Satpura ranges, and Bandhavgarh in the Vindhyas, are all tiger reserves. Though official tiger numbers are high, conservationists fear there are far fewer tigers actually.

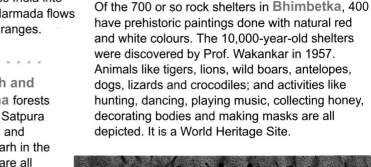

In 1857, the British explorer Captain James Forsyth spotted **Panchmarhi**, a green, saucer-shaped valley in the Satpura range. The rock shelters of Mahadeo Hill here have cave paintings, the earliest of which are 10,000 years old. There are five ancient rock shelters here which are known as the Pandava Caves.

The rounded Sanchi Hill near Bhopal has the **Great Stupa**, one of the oldest Stupas in the world. It was built by Emperor Ashoka. It has four gateways called toranas carved with stories from the Jatakas. The Stupa was forgotten till General Taylor stumbled upon it in 1818. It is now a World Heritage Site.

Central

Kaliadeh Palace, or the water palace of Ujjain, is located on an island on the River Shipra. It was built in 1458 by Nasir-ud-din Khilji. In this ingenious palace, river water was diverted in and out of the building to generate cool breezes.

An 8th century Rajput chieftain called Suraj Sen was cured of leprosy when **Gwalipa**, a hermit, asked him to drink water from a pond. In gratitude, Suraj Sen built a fort-city there and named it 'Gwalior' after the hermit.

Bhopal is situated on the site of an 11th century city called 'Bhojapal' built by Raja Bhoj. He is said to have built the lakes around which the city grew. In 1723, Dost Mohammed, an Afghan commander of the Mughals, built parts of the present city. Bhopal was ruled by four brave and wise queens or Begums from 1819 to 1926.

RAJASTHAN ☞

MADHYA PRADESH ☞

The singer Tansen was one of the nine gems of Emperor Akbar's court. A **tamarind tree** grows near his tomb in Gwalior. People believe that eating its leaves will make their voices sweeter! Legend has it that K L Saigal, the famous singer, chewed a few.

One half of **Bhawani Mandi station** on the Mumbai-Delhi railway line lies in MP and the other half lies in Rajasthan!

Arts & Crafts

Communities like the Gonds and Pradhans have a rich tradition of making wall paintings or **bhittichitras**. Bhils paint bright Pithora paintings related to creation myths. Korkus and Seherias also paint in unique and distinctive styles.

The Chippas or **hand-block printers** of Bagh use vegetable colours and intricately carved blocks with geometric and floral patterns. The block printers of Javad use blocks with the amba butti or mango motif.

Gwalior has a special tradition of making **battubai dolls**, which are dressed in traditional clothes made of paper, with tin-foil, beads and spangles as decorations.

Fact File

- **Date of formation:** November 1, 1956
  Size: 3,08,000 sq km
  Population: 60,348,023
  Capital: Bhopal
- **Rivers:** Narmada, Tapti, Betwa, Son, Chambal
  Forests and NPs: Bandhavgarh NP, Kanha NP, Pench NP, Indrawati Tiger Reserve, Kheoni WS

Language: Hindi
Neighbours: Maharashtra, Gujarat, Rajasthan, Uttar Pradesh, Chhattisgarh
State Animal: Swamp deer
State Bird: Paradise fly-catcher

Chhattisgarh

Chhattisgarh was once tucked into the southeastern corner of Madhya Pradesh. It has a proud tribal tradition and around **40%** of India's forests. There are ancient underground caves and many waterfalls like Chitrakot, which is an awesome **100** ft deep and **1000** ft wide. Chhattisgarh lies near the Maikala and Dandakaranya mountain ranges. The River Mahanadi flows through the state.

The region around present-day Chhattisgarh was ruled by the **Haihaya** dynasty till they split around the 14th century. By about the 16th century, they ruled under the Mughals. The Kakatiyas established their kingdom in Bastar from the 1320s. Marathas attacked Chhattisgarh in 1741, ending Haihaya rule. The British ruled here from 1818.

Chhattisgarh's tribes fought outsiders vigorously. Bastar's Halba rebellion (1774-1779) resisted the British and the Marathas. About eight more rebellions followed, till the **Bhumkal rebellion** of 1910, which protested against the way the tribals' traditional forest rights were being snatched from them.

Known as **Dakshin Kosala** in ancient texts, it was Ratanpur to the Mughals. The term 'Chhattisgarh' was first used in a Maratha document in 1795. Some believe the region had 36 forts, while others say it was named for the Chedi dynasty's 'garh' or fort. People also think it was named for the 36 leather-working families who moved here and set up 'chhattis ghar' or 36 houses.

Raipur

Nearly 32.5% of Chhattisgarh's population is tribal. Marias, Gonds, **Bison-horn Marias**, Baigas, Halbas, Kanars, Abhujmarias and others live here. Tribal haats or markets see produce like 'sal' butter, combs, landa or rice beer, salt, live red ants, jewellery and sulphi, or sago-palm sap.

Gonds call themselves **Koitor**—the word 'Gond' probably came from the Telugu word 'konda' or hill. Apart from the Bastar region, they also live in other places like central Madhya Pradesh. Murias, Marias and Dorlas are also Gonds. They farm, craft metal, fish and hunt. Children are trained in various skills like art and are guided towards adulthood in dormitories called Ghotul.

Bastar in southern Chhattisgarh has tribes which were living here much before the Aryans came. Around 1320, King Annam Deo of Andhra Pradesh, from the Kakatiya dynasty (a distant branch of the Chalukyas), established a princely state here. More than 70% of Bastar is tribal. Perhaps because of this, Bastar has some amazing arts and crafts.

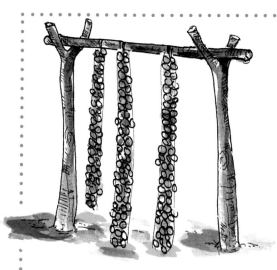

Verrier Elwin, an Oxford-educated missionary, was inspired by Rabindranath Tagore, Gandhiji and tribal ways of living. Working among Murias and Baigas, he admired their practices and the wisdom of the Ghotul system. He worked with Chhattisgarh's tribes along with his colleague Shamrao Hivale. Later, he was the advisor on Northeast tribal affairs to Jawaharlal Nehru.

The Kanger Valley is a 34-km-long transition zone where the sal forests of the north meet the teak forests of the south, with both kinds of trees growing here. Set near the River Kanger, it is one of the last patches of untouched forest left in India. The Kanger Ghati NP has tigers, flying squirrels, water birds, hill mynas, rhesus macaques, insects, butterflies, fungi and algae.

The ancient caves of Kotamsar, Kailash and Dandak in the Kanger forest have stunning limestone formations or stalagmites and stalactites. The 200-m-long, 55-m-deep Kailash has huge formations, while the pitch dark Kotamsar caves also have blind fish. The large, smooth-floored Dandak cave is set in a hillock.

The Kosa fabric of the Bastar tribals comes from the Kosa worm cocoons that grow wild here. The yarn is woven into soft saris and shawls using ancient looms. Later the fabrics are hand-printed using a natural dye called aal. Kosa is also woven in Madhya Pradesh and Orissa.

Of the approximately 90 languages and dialects that used to be spoken here, many are dying out for lack of speakers. Chhattisgarh's languages are from three important language families: Chhattisgarhi, Hindi, Marathi, Oriya, Sadri and Halbi are Indo-Aryan languages; Korku, Kharia and Korba are Munda languages; and Kurukh and Gondi are Dravidian languages.

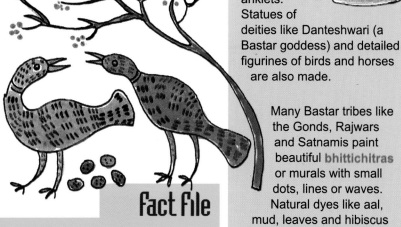

Arts & Crafts

Iron crafting is done by Lohars of Kondagoan and other parts of Bastar. The scrap that is left over while making farming tools and household goods is heated and crafted into deities, tribal soldiers, horses, pigs and different birds using the hammer. No nails or joints are used. The figurines are stark and elegant.

The lost wax method of metal casting is common in Orissa, Jharkhand, Bengal and Andhra Pradesh. In Chhattisgarh, Ghadwas use it to craft bell metal into objects like nose-pins and anklets. Statues of deities like Danteshwari (a Bastar goddess) and detailed figurines of birds and horses are also made.

Many Bastar tribes like the Gonds, Rajwars and Satnamis paint beautiful bhittichitras or murals with small dots, lines or waves. Natural dyes like aal, mud, leaves and hibiscus flowers are used. The paintings are of three kinds: brown-coloured Jagar or religious paintings; colourful, imaginative Ghotul paintings; and the vivid Madia Khamba, or the painted biography of a dead person.

Fact File

Date of formation: November 1, 2000
Size: 1,36,034 sq km
Population: 20,833,803
Capital: Raipur
Rivers: Mahanadi, Indravati, Son, Pairi, Hasdo, Sabari
Forests and NPs: Kankerghati NP, Indravati NP, Kanger Valley NP

Languages: Hindi, Oriya, Marathi, Chhattisgarhi, Gondi, Korku
Neighbours: Madhya Pradesh, Jharkhand, Uttar Pradesh, Andhra Pradesh, Orissa
State Animal: Wild buffalo
State bird: Hill myna
State tree: Sal

Gujarat

Gujarat probably got its name from the Gurjaras (possibly a Hun tribe) who lived here between the 8th and the 9th centuries AD. Many peoples and cultures have blended here—the Ahirs, Mutwas and the nomadic Rabaris, Parsis and perhaps even Greeks, who called the port of Bharuch 'Barygaza'.

The **Harappan Civilisation** prospered at Lothal or 'the mound of the dead' and Dholavira in Kutchch. Lothal was populated around 2400 BC, and had a port, a dockyard, good drainage, streets, an acropolis (a high walled city), warehouses and a bead-making industry. Dholavira was occupied from 2900 BC to 2100 BC. It had an excellent rainwater harvesting system.

You can climb down into the richly-carved **step wells** or vavs of Gujarat. Found only in the water-starved parts of northwest India, vavs offered shelter from the heat, while storing water. Rani-ki-vav, a World Heritage Site, was built by Queen Udayamati in Patan, around the 11th century AD. Adalaj vav, near Ahmedabad, was built in 1499 by Queen Rudabai.

Gandhinagar

Gujarat was ruled at different times by the Mauryas, **Kshatrapas**, Guptas, Maitrakas, Gurjaras, Solankis, Vaghelas and Alauddin Khalji, a Delhi Sultan. Mughal rule began towards the late 1500s and continued till the mid-1700s, when the Marathas took over. The British ruled here from 1818.

When the Sassanid Empire ended in Persia (modern Iran), many Zoroastrians or **Parsis** fled to India between AD 700 to 900. According to the *Qissa-i-Sanjan*, Jadi Rana, a local ruler agreed to shelter them if they adopted local ways and gave up arms. Fire is sacred to Parsis and is worshipped in a fire temple or agiary. Udvada, Surat and Navsari have Atash Behrams, the most sacred ritual fires.

In 1299, **Alauddin Khalji** made Gujarat a part of the Delhi Sultanate. Later, Gujarat's governor, Zafar Khan Muzaffar set up the Muzaffarid dynasty here. Sultan Ahmed Shah of the Muzaffarids built the city of Ahmedabad in 1411. It is believed that he chose the spot for his capital because he saw a fearless hare chase a dog here.

Sultan Ahmed Shah built beautiful monuments like the **Teen Darwaja** and the Jama Masjid. Ahmedabad's other monuments like the Shaking Minarets of the Siddi Bashir mosque, and the Siddi Sayyed mosque with its 10 semi-circular, intricately-carved windows, are also remarkable.

Junagadh, a historical city near the Girnar range, has an ancient fort called **Uparkot** which was first built by the Mauryas. It has step wells and two massive Egyptian guns. There are three groups of rock-cut caves nearby, excavated between the 1st and 4th centuries AD. Ashoka's moral rules were inscribed on a boulder here around 250 BC.

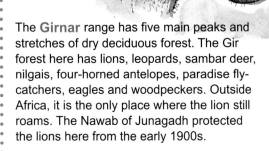

The **Girnar** range has five main peaks and stretches of dry deciduous forest. The Gir forest here has lions, leopards, sambar deer, nilgais, four-horned antelopes, paradise fly-catchers, eagles and woodpeckers. Outside Africa, it is the only place where the lion still roams. The Nawab of Junagadh protected the lions here from the early 1900s.

The dry, salt desert of the **Little Rann of Kutchch** turns into a wetland after the rains. It has a fragile ecosystem, with many species of plankton, spiders, molluscs and reptiles. Greater flamingos nest here. The khud or wild ass is a fast animal, sturdy enough to withstand heat and drought. It is protected in the Wild Ass Sanctuary here.

The colourful and rhythmic Garba is performed by a circle of clapping women. **Raas** is performed by men and women holding sticks. There are nearly 36 varieties of both the dances. Gujarat also has tribal dances like the Siddi Dhamal, the Dang and the Mer dances.

The **Marine NP** in the Gulf of Kutchch preserves a unique marine ecosystem across its 30 to 40 islands. It has coral reefs, mudflats, many mangrove species, sea grasses, seaweeds, sponges, turtles, sea snakes, birds, and 108 kinds of green and red algae.

Mahatma Gandhi (1869-1948), who was born in Porbandar, believed in non-violent civil disobedience as a form of protest. In 1930, he marched to the salt pans of Dandi in Navsari, Surat. There, on April 6, he broke the Salt Act and made illegal salt. This brought international attention to India's demands and sparked off a massive civil disobedience movement.

Bhavai, the folk theatre of Gujarat, was started in the 1300s by Asait Thakore, a brahmin who had been ostracised. He wrote 360 veshas or playlets. Bhavai uses music, dance, stories and humour to discuss social problems. Copper pipes called bhungal, pakhawaja drums, cymbals, sarangi and the harmonium accompany the performance.

Young Koli, Charan, Rabari, Kanbi, Kathi, Khant and Bharwad tribals come to the **Tarnetar** fair to find themselves brides and grooms every year. Men embroider jackets and umbrellas to carry to the fair. A girl who likes a man's needlework well enough to marry him will stand under his umbrella!

Arts & Crafts

The Muslim Khatri community of Kutchch makes the delightful **bandhani** or tie-and-dye fabric. Numerous little knots called bheendi are tied on cloth using wax thread, forming patterns of squares, circles and waves. The cloth is dipped in vats of dark, natural dyes. When the knots are opened, the tied parts are left uncoloured.

Patan's weavers use a complicated double ikat weave to create the gorgeous **Patola** fabric. Traditionally, there were different designs for Muslim Voras, Marathi brahmins, Indonesian royals, and a common one for Jains and Hindus. It takes a day to weave eight inches of patola, and six months to weave an entire sari.

Gujarat's Rabari tribals create artistic, rich **embroidery**. Ahirs sew peacocks and elephants, with the kanta or thorn stitch and mirrors. Soof embroidery of the Sodhas, Rajputs and Megwars is geometric. Mutwas work the mukko and chopat. The Jat Garasiya and Fakirani styles are also distinctive.

Fact File

- **Date of formation:** May 1, 1960
  Size: 1,96,024 sq km
  Population: 50,671,017
  Capital: Gandhinagar
- **Rivers:** Sabarmati, Mahi, Narmada, Tapti, Banas, Saraswati, Damanganga
  Forests and NPs: Gir NP, Wild Ass Sanctuary Kutchch, Nal Sarovar Bird Sanctuary, Velavadhar NP, Vansda NP

Language: Gujarati
Neighbours: National: Rajasthan, Maharashtra, Madhya Pradesh, Daman and Diu, Dadra and Nagar Haveli; **International:** Pakistan
State Animal: Asiatic lion
State Bird: Greater flamingo

Maharashtra

Maharashtra has starkly beautiful geography which lends itself to many man-made and natural wonders. The volcanic basaltic rocks in the Sahayadri Hills, for example, were softer when dug out and carved, but hardened after being exposed to the wind and the sun. They were perfect for the breathtaking rock sculpture carved here. Of the **1200** or so rock-cut temples in the state, **900** are Buddhist.

Hsuan-Tsang, the Chinese traveller-pilgrim, passed through the region around AD 640 and called it **Maholeska**. 'Maharashtra' probably came from the Maharashtri language spoken here (from which Marathi evolved); or from the tribe of great chariot builders and riders or 'maharathis' who settled down here.

The **Satavahanas** who spoke Maharashtri, Vakatakas, Kalachuris, Rashtrakutas, Chalukyas and Yadavas ruled here. From 1307, different Muslim dynasties like the Khaljis, Tughlaqs, Bahmanis and the Shahs ruled the region.

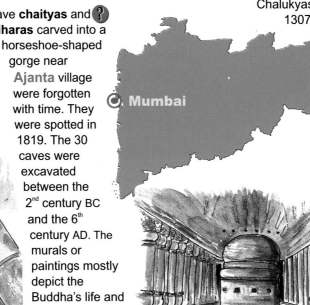

The cave **chaityas** and **viharas** carved into a horseshoe-shaped gorge near **Ajanta** village were forgotten with time. They were spotted in 1819. The 30 caves were excavated between the 2nd century BC and the 6th century AD. The murals or paintings mostly depict the Buddha's life and the Jataka Tales.

Karla, Bhaja and Bedsa caves lie close to one another and were probably dug out between the 3rd century BC and the 2nd century AD. Karla has a 37-m-long chaitya and Bhaja has a 17-m-long one. **Kanheri** has the most cave structures on one hill. Uniquely, it also has podhis or water cisterns to store rainwater.

On an ancient trade route lay Verul, a mountain village. Between the 6th and the 12th centuries AD, Buddhist, Brahmin and Jain caves were carved out of the mountainside. Today we know the cave temples of Verul Leni as **Ellora**. The Kalachuris, Chalukyas and the Rashtrakutas were the patrons of Ellora's rock art. Both Ajanta and Ellora are World Heritage Sites.

Gharapuri, just outside Mumbai, has seven beautiful rock-cut caves, carved between the 6th and the 7th centuries AD. A World Heritage Site, it has a 6-m-high bust of Shiva as **Trimurti**. When the Portuguese landed here, they saw a huge monolithic elephant statue and named it Ilha Elefante or the Elephanta Island.

Shivaji Bhonsle, born in 1627, used a small band of men and guerrilla tactics to beat large powerful armies. He built the Maratha Empire which would rule over much of central and western India by the 1700s. He was the first Indian ruler to build a strong navy.

Aurangzeb's son Azam Shah built a tomb for Rabia-ud-Durrani, his mother, in Aurangabad. Called **Bibi-Ka-Maqbara**, it was built between 1651 and 1661, with the help of Ataullah, an architect, and Harispat Rai, an engineer. Its dome has exquisite trellis work and floral panels.

50

The Sahyadri Hills or the **Western Ghats** rise from Gujarat and go as far as Tamil Nadu. They lie parallel to the coast and divide Maharashtra into the Konkan to the west, and 'desh' to the east. Many rivers originate from the Western Ghats.

The Dhangari Gaja of Dhangars, or shepherds; the Koli dance; povadas or ballets about bravery; Kala and Dindi are among Maharashtra's folk dances. Tamasha, a form of folk-theatre, has a devotional song, a dramatic sequence, a play and a love song or **lavani**.

Pioneers like Harishchandra Bhatvadekar made short films on monkeys and wrestlers in Mumbai. Others filmed whole plays. **Dhundiraj Govind (Dadasaheb) Phalke** made India's first feature film—*Raja Harishchandra* (1913). He made more than a 100 films in his lifetime. Mumbai today has a thriving film industry.

Forests like Chandoli, Gugamal, Navegaon, Tadoba and Pench cover about 15% of Maharashtra. The Melghat Tiger Reserve has bamboo groves, teak trees, tigers, sloth bears, and deer. The ecology of Bhimashankar WS is threatened by the many tourists and pilgrims who visit it. It is home to the **Indian giant squirrel**.

The world's largest national park within a city is Mumbai's **Sanjay Gandhi NP**. It is seriously threatened by urban growth. The park has many insects, animals and birds, and acts as Mumbai's lung.

Kolis were among the first residents of the archipelago or arc of seven islands that later became Mumbai. Kolbhat or Colaba, Old Woman's Island, Bombay, Mazagaon, Worli, Parel and Mahim were joined between 1784 and 1845. Called 'Bombaim' by the Portuguese, and Bombay by the British, the city was finally named for Mumbadevi, a Koli goddess.

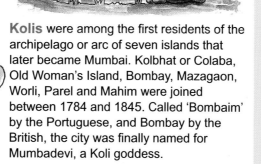

Arts & Crafts

Women of the **Warli** tribe create striking ritualistic paintings on cowdung-plastered walls, using white rice powder and bamboo twigs. These paintings are full of movement. Motifs like people, trees, peacocks, animals and social activities fill them. Jivya Soma Mashe, a Warli, first brought the form to the outside world.

Paithani saris are a blend of gold and silk, and come in splashy magenta, purple and blue. Vines, flowers, peacocks, parrots, lotuses, gold coins, mangoes and coconuts are popular motifs. The Peshwas loved the fabric, as did the Hyderabad Nizam and his daughter-in-law, Begum Niloufer, who brought in new designs for borders.

Paithan and Aurangabad are famous for **Mashru and Himroo** fabrics as well. Mashru is a woven mix of striped cotton and silk. Himroo, also a mix, is as thin as muslin, with fine silver and gold threads. It was used by royalty especially as veils.

Fact File

Date of formation: May 1, 1960
Size: 3,07,713 sq km
Population: 96,752,247
Capital: Mumbai
Rivers: Godavari, Penganga, Bhima, Varna, Parvara, Mula
Forests and NPs: Pench NP, Tadoba NP, Nagzira NP, Nawegoan NP, Devlagaon NP, Gugamal NP

Language: Marathi
Neighbours: Gujarat, Madhya Pradesh, Andhra Pradesh, Karnataka, Goa, Chhattisgarh, Dadra and Nagar Haveli
State Animal: Giant squirrel
State Bird: Green imperial pigeon
State Tree: Mango
State Flower: Jarul

Goa

Goa was first mentioned by the Sumerian King Gudea who called it 'Gubio' around 2200 BC. Gopakapatana to the Kadambas, it was Gove or Govapuri to ancient Hindus, Sindabur to Arabs, Sibo to Greeks, Guvah-Sindabur to Turks, and Goa to the Portuguese. The Sanskrit 'Gomantak' or 'fertile, well-watered land' probably best suits the emerald-green state, with its bright-red soil and its many rivers.

Though the Satavahanas were the first to rule here, Goa was also ruled by the Abhiras, Batpuras, Bhojas, Chalukyas and Rashtrakutas. Goa prospered under **Kadamba** rule from 1006 to 1356. This was followed by Bahmani rule, the Vijayanagara Empire, and finally, in 1492, by Sultan Adil Shah of Bijapur.

While Arabs had traded spices and silks freely with India for centuries, European merchants tried to control the trade. Vasco da Gama was the first Portuguese trader to land in north Kerala in 1498. **Alfonso de Albuquerque** conquered Goa in 1510. He made it a trade centre for Arab horses, and built churches and hospitals. He also tried to end Sati.

From 1948, India demanded that Portugal give up its colonies here. The United Front of Goans, led by Francis Mascarenhas, the Azad Gomantak Dal, Goan People's Party, satyagrahis and other Goan groups fought for **liberation**. Finally, Goa, Daman and Diu were liberated in 1961. Goa officially became a part of India in 1962.

Panaji

Old Goa was founded by the Bahmani and Vijayanagara kings as a port town. It was the Portuguese capital in the east. But it was abandoned after epidemics struck it in the late 1700s. The **Basilica of Bom Jesus** here holds the tomb of St Francis Xavier. The Basilica, the Se Cathedral and a few other churches here are World Heritage Sites.

Performances like the Dekhni, Zagor, Ghode Modni, Fugdi, Dhalo, Goph, Morulem Khel, Shigmo Khel, dances of Hindu and Christian Kunbis, and others, reflect Goa's history. **Muslam Khel** or the pestle dance was performed by the Kshatriyas of Chandore under Kadamba rule. Their descendants still perform the dance every February.

In the 1960s, many young people from the West set off on road trips to the East. On the way, they discovered Goa, with its unspoiled **beaches and villages**. Since then, many tourists have flooded in, putting a great strain on both the environment and the social fabric of Goa.

Goa has a 105-km-long coast. It lies between the Rivers Mandovi and Zuari. Some of the other rivers here are Terekhol, Chapora, Baga, Sal and Talpona. They form **waterways** to transport people and goods. On the Konkan coast, the Mormugao Harbour is one of the best, apart from the harbours at Mumbai and Kozhikode.

The **Tiatr** tradition of Goa is more than a hundred years old. Performed by Catholics, the sharply satirical Tiatr plays helped preserve Konkani. They are divided into six or seven acts called podd'dde. Though Lucasinho Ribeiro translated and performed the first Tiatr in 1892, it was Agostinho Fernandes who wrote the first original Konkani Tiatr.

Chorao Island's 1.8-sq-km **Dr Salim Ali Bird Sanctuary** has a network of waterways, a mangrove ecosystem, local and migratory birds, flying foxes, jackals and crocodiles. Bondla WS's moist deciduous forests have many birds, panthers, jungle cats, gaurs, and porcupines.

Panaji was originally a suburb of Old or Velha Goa. It officially became Nova Goa, the new capital, in 1843, after Old Goa was abandoned. Built on the banks of River Mandovi, it was called Ponnji, the 'land that never got flooded'. **Fontainhas**, an old pocket in the city, has narrow streets and Latin-style houses painted in colours like red, blue and yellow. The houses have clay-tiled roofs.

Fact File

Date of formation: May 30, 1987
Size: 3702 sq km
Population: 1,347,668
Capital: Panaji
Rivers: Mandovi, Zuari, Terekhol, Chapora, Sal, Talpona

Forests and NPs: Bondla WS, Morlem NP, Dr Salim Ali Bird Sanctuary, Cotigoa WS, Bhagwan Mahavir WS
Languages: Konkani, Marathi
Neighbours: Karnataka, Maharashtra
State Animal: Gaur
State Bird: Black-crested bulbul
State Tree: Asna

Arts & Crafts

The red laterite soil of Goa is worked into attractive pots, utensils, lamps, figurines and panels in **terracotta** or baked clay. Though pottery is commonly made all over Goa, the potters of Borde and Bicholim are well-known for their craftsmanship.

With the Portuguese came the craft of **crochet**. In crochet, yarn or thread is knotted using a hook and made into a net-like fabric. Tablecloths, curtains, cushion covers, hankies and clothes are made with the fabric that is patterned with web-like lace.

The knowledge of working with **cane and bamboo** is said to have been brought to Goa by the Mahar community. Bamboo and cane are used to make useful things like patlo (baskets), cane fish traps, mats for drying fish, and varli, to wash rice in.

Andhra Pradesh

Andhra Pradesh has been influenced in its practices, beliefs, art and language by religions as diverse as Buddhism, Hinduism and Islam. So when in Andhra Pradesh, don't be surprised if you run into ancient Buddhist monuments, painted Hindu scrolls and graceful Muslim architecture all at the same time!

Hyderabad ◉

The poet-king **Mohammed Quli Qutb Shah** was also a great builder. He built Hyderabad in 1591 with good roads and remarkable monuments. At its centre was the beautiful, square-shaped **Charminar**, with four roads radiating outwards. It has four tall minarets and 45 covered prayer spaces. Close to it, stands the impressive Mecca Masjid which was begun in the early 1600s.

The Salar Jung Museum was created out of just one man's collection of antiques and artifacts. **Mir Yousuf Ali Khan**

Salar Jung III (1889-1949) collected rare art objects from the West, China, Japan and India. His Indian collection includes South Indian bronze statues, Mughal miniatures, carpets, daggers and rare manuscripts. The collection is spread over 38 galleries in the museum.

The **Nehru Zoological Park**, established in 1959 across 300 acres of land, is the biggest zoo in India. Its 250 animal species are kept in as natural an environment as possible. Tigers, rhinos, Asian and African lions, otters, chimpanzees, orangutans, antelopes and deer live here.

The **Satavahanas** were an Andhra dynasty. They ruled here from the 1st century AD. They were tolerant of different religions, and encouraged architecture and literature. The Chalukyas, Kakatiyas, Bahmanis, Vijayanagara kings, Qutb Shahis, Mughals and the Asaf Jahis also ruled here.

The 3500-sq-km **Nagarjunasagar-Srisailam WS** was declared a tiger reserve in 1983. It is one of the largest tiger reserves. River Krishna, the oldest river in the country, flows through it. It has pythons, sloth bears, panthers, tigers, leopards, blackbucks, mouse deer and pangolins.

Nagarjuna Sagar Dam, built on the River Krishna in 1960, is one of the largest masonry dams in the world. The fertile valley has had people from ancient times. Remains of an old Buddhist university and viharas were found there. Before the dam could drown the ruins, archaeologists worked for six years to save them. They were reconstructed on Nagarjunakonda, an island. The ruins of the Buddhist university were shifted to Anupu nearby.

A shepherd found an idol on the granite Mangalavaram hill, inspiring the Kakatiyas to build a mud fort here around 1143. **Golconda** got its name from the Telugu words 'golla konda' or the shepherd's hill. The Qutb Shahis rebuilt it over 62 years. It had strong fortifications, diamond mines, and ingenious systems of ventilation, water supply, signalling and acoustics.

AP has fascinating **cave networks**. The limestone Borra Caves are 150 million years old. Documented in 1807 by William King George, the caves have a 300-ft-thick roof and are spread over 1 sq km underground. They are called 'borra' or 'brain' in Telugu.

Many Andhra villages make toys. In Kondapalli, toys depict village life; in Tiruchanur they are religious figures. In **Nirmal** village people make animals and birds; while in **Ettikoppaka**, they make different kinds of toys. They are painted by pressing a stick of lac on the toy while turning it on a lathe, and are called 'turned toys'.

The 3.5 km Belum cave system lies under a flat field. Robert Bruce Foote was the first to document it in 1884. In 1982, the German speleologist Herbert Daniel Gebauer explored it with the help of local people. Belum has large halls with amazing rock formations. In one hall the rock looks like the aerial root system of a **banyan tree**.

Pochampalli village has a long tradition of Ikat weaving. Here either the warp or the weft is dyed before it is woven. Cooperatives help weavers make and market the fabric.

Warangal was the capital of the Kakatiya dynasty, which patronised architecture. The Ramappa temple was built by them. Rudra Deva built the thousand-pillar temple in 1163. Apart from the 1000 intricately carved pillars, it also has a 6-ft-tall **Nandi bull** carved out of a single rock.

Kalamkari cotton is either block-printed or else painted on with a bamboo pen or kalam, using vegetable dyes. The craft probably grew out of contact with Persian traders. Sri Kalahasti in AP has been producing kalamkari cloth for centuries.

In Shivaram WS near the River Godavari, watch out for **mugger crocodiles**! These marsh crocodiles live in fresh-water. Shivaram was established in 1987 mainly to protect them. Unlike their salt-water cousins, muggers can crawl long distances. The 37-sq-km sanctuary has tigers, panthers, nilgais, pythons and monkeys.

Cured and dried goatskin is coloured with vegetable dyes to make **Tholu Bommalatta** or leather puppets. They are part of the Chaya Natak (shadow theatre) tradition. The six-to-eight-hour performances are accompanied by music and sound effects.

The Nakashis of **Cheriyal** village used to paint vibrantly-coloured scrolls. A storytelling community called Kaki Padagollu used to take these long, beautiful scrolls from village to village to help them narrate stories from the epics.

Fact File

Date of formation: November 1, 1956
Size: 2,75,069 sq km
Population: 76,210,007
Capital: Hyderabad
Rivers: Godavari, Krishna, Wainganga, Tungabhadra, Chitravati, Musi, Banda, Papagni
Forests and NPs: Shivaram WS, Manjira WS, Nagarjunasagar-Srisailam WS

Languages: Telugu, Urdu
Neighbours: Maharashtra, Chhattisgarh, Orissa, Karnataka, Tamil Nadu, Yanam (Puducherry)
State Animal: Blackbuck
State Bird: Indian roller
State Tree: Neem

Karnataka

or Karunadu—the high land—was ruled by dynasties like the Mauryas, Kadambas, Western Gangas, Pallavas, Chalukyas, Rashtrakutas, Hoysalas, Bahmanis, Vijayanagaras, Mughals, Wodeyars and Tipu Sultan. Each built splendid monuments which stand even today like markers of history.

The Hoysalas ruled a little after the Chalukyas. Under their chieftain Bittiga, later called Vishnuvardhan, they built low, intricate, star-shaped temples. The Hoysaleshwara temple in their capital **Halebidu** was built around AD 1121.

In **Belur**, another Hoysala city, Vishnuvardhan built the large and carefully detailed Chennakeshava temple in the 12th century probably to celebrate his victory over the Cholas.

Bengaluru

With the end of the Hoysala Empire, the Delhi sultans took over briefly. A chieftain called Sangama and his sons, Harihara and Bukka, fought them and built the Vijayanagara Empire (1336-1614). Their last capital, **Hampi**, has beautiful temples and is a World Heritage Site. The Bahmani Sultanate of Bidar, founded by Ala-al-Din Bahman Shah in 1347, reached its peak between 1466 and 1481.

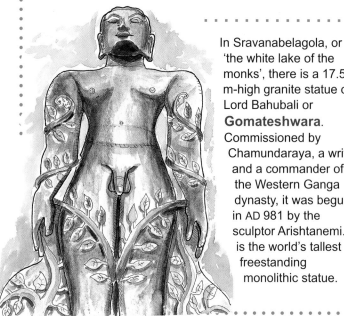

In Sravanabelagola, or 'the white lake of the monks', there is a 17.5-m-high granite statue of Lord Bahubali or **Gomateshwara**. Commissioned by Chamundaraya, a writer and a commander of the Western Ganga dynasty, it was begun in AD 981 by the sculptor Arishtanemi. It is the world's tallest freestanding monolithic statue.

The **Chalukyas** experimented with temple-building styles in Aihole, their first capital. They combined the southern or Dravida style of temple-building with the northern Nagara style, to create the new Vesara style. They built many temples between the 6th and 12th centuries.

Pattadakal—the second Chalukyan capital—was where their art was perfected. The complex of 10 temples here is a World Heritage Site. The Virupaksha temple built by Queen Trilokyamahadevi around AD 740 is most beautiful.

In Badami, the Chalukyas carved cave temples out of the soft red local sandstone. They built freestanding temples here too. Of the four cave temples in Badami, the first is devoted to Shiva as the 18-armed **Nataraja** in different dance poses. The other three are devoted to Vishnu and Jain Tirthankaras.

The **Gol Gumbaz** of Bijapur was Muhammad Adil Shah's (ruled from 1627-1656) tomb. It took 20 years to build. At 37.92 m, its central dome is the second largest in the world. It has a whispering gallery and a huge central hall.

The fiercely independent **Haider Ali** interrupted Wodeyar rule over the region. He organised the first Indian-controlled army of 30 armed European soldiers and rose in power within the Mysore government. In 1761, he made himself king. Both he and his son Tipu Sultan resisted British expansion in South India.

Haider's son, **Fateh Ali Tipu** (1750-1799), was called the 'Tiger of Mysore'. He was brave, tolerant and farsighted. He built roads, dams and ports; and developed Karnataka's silk industry by getting silkworms from Bengal and starting 21 silk centres. He had a collection of unique objects like **'Tipu's Tiger'** an automatic musical organ which showed a tiger attacking a British soldier. In 1881, the British gave the kingdom of Mysore to the Wodeyars.

Ibrahim Adil Shah II (1580-1627) built **Ibrahim Rauza**, a tomb for his wife Taj Sultana. The tomb's graceful and delicately-carved minarets may have inspired those of the Taj Mahal.

Bandipur NP became a part of Project Tiger in 1973. It falls in the Niligiri Biosphere Reserve (NBR) which covers seven forests in South India. Bandipur has evergreen forests, grasslands, tigers, elephants, bison, barking deer and the nocturnal porcupine.

Nagarhole NP, also a part of the NBR, has swamps and snake-like streams. It also has flying foxes, jungle cats, bonnet macaques, black-naped hares, panthers and 250 bird species.

Tuluvas and the **Kodavas** of Coorg have distinctive practices and dress. Karnataka is also home to tribes like the Bedars, Jenu Kurubas, Todas, Soligas, Yeravas, Siddis, Kadu Kurubas and others. Tibetan refugees have lived here since 1961.

Yakshagana, or the 'celebration of celestial beings' is a form of folk theatre. Travelling troupes combine song, dance and drama to retell epics. They are accompanied by drums called chande and tala or cymbals.

Fact File

Date of formation: November 1, 1973
Size: 1,91,791 sq km
Population: 52,850,562
Capital: Bangalore
Rivers: Krishna, Tungabhadra, Cauvery, Kabini
Forests and NPs: Bandipur WS, Nagarhole NP, Mudumalai NP
Languages: Kannada, Kodava, Tulu

Neighbours: Goa, Kerala, Andhra Pradesh, Maharashtra, Tamil Nadu
State Animal: Elephant
State Bird: Indian roller
State Tree: Sandal
State Flower: Lotus

Arts & Crafts

In Chennapatana, **Chitragars** chisel wood and then turn it on a wooden lathe to smoothen and lacquer it. In Gokak, Jingar craftsmen make fruit-and-vegetable sets using a painstaking 200-year-old process.

The ancient craft of **Bidri** came from Persia to Bidar during the Bahmani rule. The craft uses an object made of a metal alloy as the base. A design is engraved on it and silver wire is inlaid into it. Finally it is heated and rubbed with mud taken from the Bidri fort, which turns it jet black.

The ancient card game of **Ganjifa** was popular with royalty across India. Beautiful cards were made in Orissa, Andhra Pradesh, Maharashtra and Bengal. Mysore's Krishnaraja Wodeyar III designed a version called Chad. The cards were painted on handmade paper with natural dyes and then lacquered.

Kerala

Kerala was known in the ancient world for its pepper and its ports. An Ashokan rock inscription from the 3rd century BC first mentions it as 'Keralaputra'. Kathiayana, Patanjali and Megasthenes also wrote about it. Traders from Egypt, Asia Minor, China, Greece, Rome, Philippines, Java, Sumatra and West Asia came here, creating a blend of religions, languages and cultures.

Jews settled in Kerala as early as the 1st century AD. Some fled here to escape persecution, while others came as traders. The Mattancherry or Kochi or Paradesi Synagogue was built in 1568 by King Raja Rama Varma after the Portuguese destroyed an older one. Built next to the palace temple, it has beautiful glass chandeliers and a clock tower.

King Cheraman Perumal learnt about Prophet Mohammed from Malik Ibn Dinar, an Arab trader, in the 7th century AD. He travelled to Jeddah to meet the Prophet. The **Cheraman Malik Masjid** in Kodangallur is the oldest mosque in India. It was built in AD 629 by Dinar with help from local rulers.

Wayanad WS is made up of two forests and is part of the Nilgiri Biosphere Reserve (NBR). Many of NBR's tribals—**Paniyans**, Kattunayakans, Kurichyas, Adiyas and Uralikurumbars—live here. The Kurichyas are great archers and helped the rebel Pazhassi Raja wage a guerilla war against the British in the 1800s.

Edakkal caves in Ambukutty Mountain, Wayanad, have petroglyphs or **rock carvings** believed to be made by **Neolithic** man. Edakkal means 'a stone in between' and was actually a cleft created by an earthquake. Fred Fawcett first spotted the two-level caves in 1890.

Kerala was ruled by Tamil dynasties like the Pandyas, Cholas and Cheras, till the **Kulashekhara dynasty** took over. It developed a distinct regional identity from Tamil Nadu between the 8th and 14th centuries AD. Malayalam grew away from Tamil around the same time.

St Thomas, an Apostle of Jesus, probably travelled on a trading boat from Alexandria to Kerala in AD 52. Many people converted to Christianity under him. Since their prayers used Syriac words, they were called 'Syrian Christians'.

With around 44 rivers, Kerala has a 900-km network of **lakes and lagoons**. They are a means of transport, farming and fishing. Estuaries are formed wherever river water meets the salty Arabian Sea. This mix of waters has created a unique ecosystem.

Thiruvananthapuram

People and goods were ferried through the waterways in grain barges called **kettuvallams** or 'tied boats'. Made with sturdy anjili wood, they were tied so tightly with coir that they did not need nails.

Chundan vallams, or the unsinkable, lip-shaped, snake boats, can be more than 100 ft long. Each boat is about 20 ft high at the back, making it look like a snake with a raised hood. A chundan vallam belongs to a village and is worshipped. During boat races, oarsmen sit in pairs, singing zestfully and rowing in rhythm.

The energetic and vibrant **Theyyam** is performed by the Panan, Velan and Vannan communities. Dance, music and pre-brahminical rites make up the 12-hour performances held in sacred groves or kavus. The Mother Goddess, ancestors, heroes, animals and snakes are worshipped.

Eravikulam NP has a large population of the endangered Nilgiri tahr. It has the shola-grassland type of ecosystem. The **neelakurunji** shrub flowers once in 12 years covering the hills in a blue blaze.

Unlike most forests, noisy cicadas don't buzz in the Silent Valley NP. Part of the NBR, it has the endangered **lion-tailed macaque**. Since 1928, there have been plans to convert it into a site for a hydroelectric project. It was finally declared an NP in 1984, thanks to efforts by conservationists.

In **Kalamezhuthu**, ritual pictures or kalams of deities are drawn on temple floors or in sacred groves, using only five vegetable colours. Artists sing songs and follow fixed steps while drawing a kalam. Finally it is worshipped and erased.

Recognised by UNESCO as a Masterpiece of the Oral and Intangible Heritage of Humanity, the 2000-year-old **Koodiyattam** is performed by members of the Chakyar caste in a koothambalam, or special part of the temple.

Kathakali is a form of dance that tells stories. Performers use elaborate make up, costumes, facial movements and vigorous steps. Make up varies according to the character's nature: green signifies nobility; black is for demonesses and hunters; minuku, the 'pretty' look, is for women; villains have the katti or 'knife' look.

Murals in Kerala's temples and churches were painted between the 9th and 15th centuries AD. In keeping with the ancient text *Silparatnam*, only 'pure' colours like white, ochre, red, black and green were used.

Raja Ravi Varma (1848-1906) was trained by his uncle, Raja Raja Varma, and by Rama Swamy Naidu, Arumugham Pillai and Thomas Jenson. His paintings were very popular and even inspired the filmmaker Dadasaheb Phalke. Varma's sister Mangalabai was also a painter and sometimes assisted him.

Believed to be the oldest of all martial forms, **Kalaripayattu** gets its name from 'kalari' meaning 'school' and 'payattu' meaning 'practice'. Kalari fighters are trained in four steps: flexibility, fighting with sticks, then metal weapons, and finally, fighting with bare hands.

Bell metal, an alloy of copper, brass and tin, is used to make idols, nilavillakkus or standing lamps and thookavillakkus or hanging lamps. Bell-metal vessels or 'urlis' can be up to 6 ft wide. In Aranmula, exquisite mirrors are made using an alloy of copper and tin.

Fact File

Date of formation: November 1, 1956
Size: 38,863 sq km
Population: 31,841,374
Capital: Thiruvananthapuram
Rivers: Periyar, Bharathapuzha
Forests and Nps: Periyar NP, Wayanad NP, Silent Valley NP

Language: Malayalam
Neighbours: Tamil Nadu, Karnataka, Mahe, Lakshwadweep
State Animal: Elephant
State Bird: Great Indian hornbill
State Tree: Coconut
State Flower: Kanikonna or Indian laburnum or amaltas

Tamil Nadu

has a history that goes far back, to powerful dynasties, ancient literary academies, rock-cut monuments, temples and churches. In 1640, the East India Company built a trading post in Madraspattanam, a fishing village. It grew to become the Madras Presidency, from which modern Andhra Pradesh, Kerala, Karnataka and Tamil Nadu were carved out after 1953.

Tamil is a classical language like Sanskrit. Many Tamil poems and plays were written during the Sangams or literary academies, probably held between the 1st and the 4th centuries AD. Sangam literature has collections of secular, non-religious poetry like *Tolkappiyam* and *Ettuttokai*. The Alvar and Nayanar saint-poets of the 7th to the 10th centuries began the Bhakti movement by writing passionate poetry about gods. The movement slowly spread to north India.

Chennai

The land of Tamilakam (which included parts of present-day Kerala) was ruled by three powerful dynasties: the Cheras, Cholas and Pandyas. Around the 6th century AD, other dynasties like the Pallavas emerged. From the late 14th century, the Vijayanagara Empire took over, and ruled here for 300 years.

Silappathikaram or *The Jewelled Anklet*, was a long epic love poem written by the Chera saint-prince Ilango Adigal between the 5th and 6th centuries AD. Its dramatic story was probably based on an older folktale. It describes town planning, cities, dance, music and the mingling of Greeks, Arabs and Tamils on city streets.

Influenced by the 11th century AD Tamil version of the *Ramayana* by Kamban, Umaru Pulavar, a 17th century poet, wrote *Cira puranam*, a poetic life of Prophet Mohammed in Tamil. Pulavar's descriptions of Arabia mirror TN's beauty, with its lush paddy fields and heavy rains.

Bharatanatyam was described in Bharata Muni's *Natya Shastra*, probably written before the 1st century AD. Called dasi-attam, it was traditionally performed by temple dancers or devadasis. In the late 1800s, four brothers who were dancers—Chinniyah, Ponniah, Sivanandam and Vadivelu—revived the form by studying it in ancient texts and on temple sculptures. Rukmini Devi Arundale was the first to perform the dance on stage in the 1930s.

TN has many folk dances like karagattam, mayilattam, oyilattam, poykkal kuthiraiyattam, kummi, kavadi attam and maanattam. In mayilattam, dancers dress like peacocks; in maanattam, they mimic deer; while in poykkal kuthiraiyattam, they mimic horses.

Mamallapuram is a group of rock-cut monuments and temples carved between the 7th and 8th centuries AD in Mahabalipuram. It was named after the Pallava king Narasimhavarman whose title was 'Mamalla'. Its cave shelters (mandapas), monolithic chariot-temples and a relief sculpture known as the 'Descent of Ganga' are remarkable. It is now a World Heritage Site.

Entire towns have grown around magnificent Tamil temples like the **Meenakshi** temple at Madurai, which was built by the Pandyas. The Brihadeeshwara, Airavateshwara, Chidambaram and Rameshwaram temples are also spectacular.

Chennai's **film industry** is prolific. Fan clubs and temples are dedicated to actors. Chief Ministers like M G Ramachandran and J Jayalalithaa were once actors. Rajinikanth is currently one of the most popular stars.

Vailankanni town has the church of **Our Lady of Good Health**, a place of pilgrimage for Catholics. Mother Mary is supposed to have appeared here miraculously in the 1500s. A small chapel was built here then. Later, a grander, Gothic-style church was built.

In 1986, forests of the Nilgiri mountain range in Karnataka, Tamil Nadu and Kerala became a part of a network called the **Nilgiri Biosphere Reserve**. It covers 5520 sq km and has seven NPs within it. The largest portion is in TN. Its shola-grassland ecosystem has dense evergreen forests separated by grassy hills. Todas, Irulas, Paniyas, Mullukurumbas, Kattunaikans, Badagas and Kotas live here.

Romulus Whitaker set up the Madras Crocodile Bank in 1976 to save the three endangered Indian crocodile species: muggers, saltwater crocodiles and gharials. Inspired by the Irulas' knowledge of snakes, he helped them form a cooperative to preserve it. He won the Whitley Award for Leadership in Nature Conservation.

Arts & Crafts

The Maratha general Venkoji conquered Thanjavur in 1676. The Thanjavur or **Tanjore style** of painting developed during the 200 years of Maratha rule that followed. It was done on wooden board with gold leaf, tamarind paste and gemstones. Popular subjects were baby Krishna's pranks or Rama's coronation.

The thick, colourful, mulberry silks of **Kanchipuram** are considered family heirlooms. The border, the body and the pallu of the sari are woven separately, and then joined with an extra-strong weave. The 400-year-old industry traditionally uses designs like checks, parrots, swans, peacocks, the sun and the moon.

Toda women of the Nilgiris embroider geometrical patterns on long shawls called poothkuli. The embroidery, called 'pugar' or 'flower', is so closely-done that it resembles a weave. Flowers are a common motif, and so are buffalo-horns, since the buffalo is sacred to the Todas.

Fact File

Date of formation: August 15, 1947
Size: 1,30,058 sq km
Population: 62,405,679
Capital: Chennai
Rivers: Kaveri, Palar, Pniyar, Bhavani
Forests and NPs: Mudumalai NP, Mukurthi NP, Annamalai NP

Language: Tamil
Neighbours: Kerala, Karnataka, Andhra Pradesh
State Animal: Nilgiri tahr
State Bird: Emerald dove
State Tree: Palmera palm
State Flower: Glory lily or Kandhal

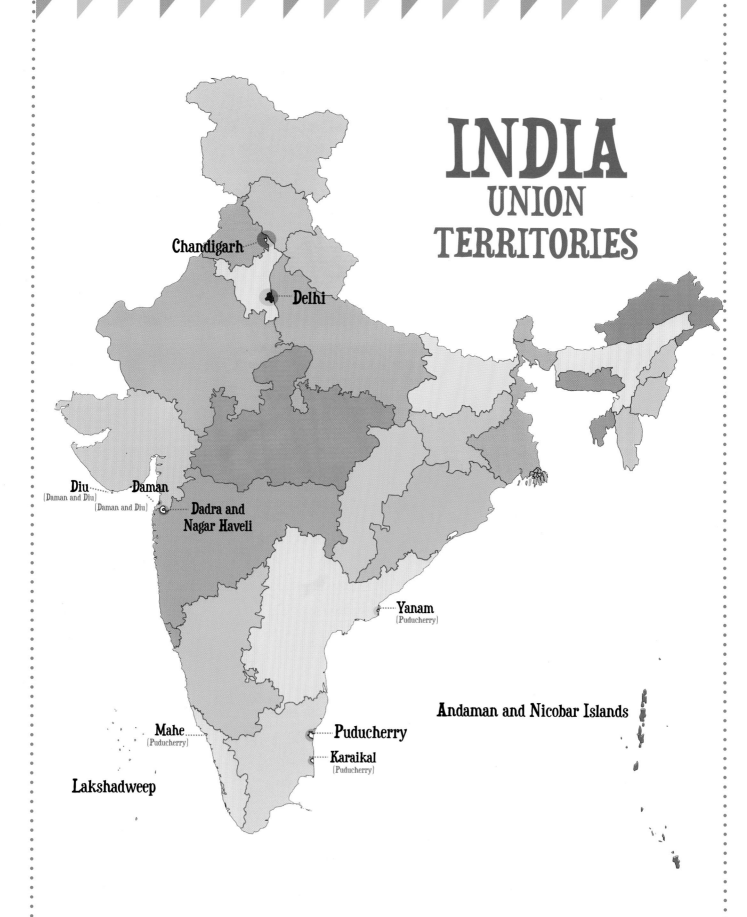

INDIA
UNION
TERRITORIES

Chandigarh

Delhi

Diu
[Daman and Diu]

Daman
[Daman and Diu]

Dadra and
Nagar Haveli

Yanam
(Puducherry)

Andaman and Nicobar Islands

Mahe
(Puducherry)

Puducherry

Karaikal
(Puducherry)

Lakshadweep

Delhi

Delhi is set near the rocky Aravalli range and probably got its name from its 1st century BC ruler Raja Dhilu. It became the capital of British India in 1912. Because it was part of many kingdoms, Delhi has amazing monuments and ruins. The Pandavas' legendary capital, Indraprastha, supposedly stood here in 1400 BC. But actual Mauryan ruins found here date only as far back as 300 BC.

Delhi's awe-inspiring monuments include a 22-ft-tall iron pillar (AD 375-415); Jama Masjid, India's largest mosque (1655); the Purana Qila; Jantar Mantar and the India Gate. Delhi has three World Heritage Sites: the **Qutub Minar** begun by Qutbuddin Aybak in 1193, Humayun's tomb built in 1570, and the Red Fort built by Shah Jahan in 1639. Humayun's tomb was the first to be built with a garden in India. It inspired many more such monuments, including the Taj Mahal.

It is believed that Delhi was destroyed and re-built at least seven times within a triangular area of about 180 sq km. Shah Jahan began to re-build it in 1639 as Shahjahanabad. Called **Old Delhi** now, it had defences like the Ajmeri, Delhi and Kashmiri Gates.

Distinct from Old Delhi's small lanes and blind alleys, are **New Delhi's** wide, tree-lined roads. Set on Raisina Hill, it was planned by Edwin Lutyens and built between 1912 and 1931. The Rashtrapati Bhavan was one of the many administrative buildings designed by Lutyens. Herbert Baker designed the Parliament House.

To the Mughals, a **garden** was a piece of paradise. Delhi has the Lodi Gardens around the Lodi kings' tombs, Roshanara Bagh built by Aurangzeb's sister, Shalimar Gardens and Talkatora Gardens. Lutyens designed the Mughal Gardens. One of them, the Circular Garden, is also called the Butterfly Garden because it attracts many butterflies.

Delhi is a state that is also administered by the centre. Known as the **National Capital Territory**, it is part of the National Capital Region which includes a few districts from Haryana, Uttar Pradesh and Rajasthan. It was planned in 1962 to reduce Delhi's congestion. It is one of the world's largest urban clusters.

Fact File

Date of formation: December 1991
Size: 1483 sq km
Population: 1,38,50,507
Capital: Delhi
River: Yamuna
Languages: Hindi, Punjabi, Urdu
Neighbours: Haryana, Uttar Pradesh

Chandigarh

Chandigarh is the capital of both Punjab and Haryana. It was planned and built from scratch as an example of the clean and green cities that India aspired to have. Chandigarh has many small, large and medium scale industries.

Jawaharlal Nehru commissioned Albert Mayer to build a new city as a symbol of modern India. Later the French architect Charles-Édouard Jeanneret or **Le Corbusier** took over, planning the city with tree-lined streets, large open spaces, terraced houses, official buildings and flower gardens.

With Lahore, the capital of undivided Punjab, going to Pakistan, an area of 114 sq km in the foothills of the Shivaliks was identified as the site for a new capital. One of the villages in the area had a temple to Goddess Chandi, and lent its name—**Chandigarh**—to the new capital.

Punjab's capital was officially shifted from Shimla to Chandigarh in September 1953. When Haryana split from Punjab in 1966, the states continued to share a capital. Chandigarh then became a **Union Territory**.

Union Territories

Around 1965, Nek Chand, a Roads Inspector, cleared a small patch of jungle and began making whimsical statues using scrap—rocks, stones, broken bangles, sockets, pottery, forks, industrial waste and cycle parts. Soon his 'scrapture' was discovered, and though it went against the rules of the planned city, authorities decided to let him expand his Rock Garden to its current 40 acres.

The Shivalik foothills where Chandigarh stands once had fruit groves and two powerful seasonal streams—**Sukhna Choe and Patialiki Rao**. The Sukhna was dammed and an artificial rainwater-fed lake was built. Sukhna WS has about 30 species of local and migratory birds. Unchecked construction around the lake has led to silting in the water. Fewer birds visit it now.

Fact File

Date of formation: Declared a Union Territory in 1966
Size: 114 sq km
Population: 9,00,635
Capital: Chandigarh
Forests and NPs: Sukhna Lake WS
Languages: Hindi, Punjabi, English
Neighbours: Punjab, Haryana

Daman & Diu
are in fact two districts clubbed together under one Union Territory, and are far from one another. Daman is located near Gujarat and Dadra; while Diu is an island off the Kathiawar Peninsula. Important for sea trade, both were ruled by old Indian empires, local rulers, Sultans and Shahs, and the Portuguese.

King Jallandhar of **Diu**, a just ruler, was said to have been killed by Vishnu. The king is still worshipped here. The Mauryas ruled here between 322 BC and 320 BC, followed by the Kshatrapas, Guptas, Maitrakas, Chavdas, Chalukyas, Rajputs, Delhi Sultans and the Shahs of Gujarat. The Portuguese captured this important naval base in 1535.

Daman was once a part of the Kushana Empire. It was also ruled by Kshatrapas, Satavahanas and Rashtrakutas. A Rajput prince called Ramsingh defeated the Koli ruler and made it a part of the Ramnagar kingdom in 1262. From the 1400s, the Shahs of Gujarat ruled it. The Portuguese conquered it in 1559. Daman and Diu were both liberated in 1961.

Sandy, marshy Diu is an island off the southern coast of the Kathiawar Peninsula in Gujarat. A creek separates the peninsula from Diu. It has beautiful beaches like Jallandhar and Nagoa, and an ancient fort called **Panikot**. The Cathedral of St Matriz here was built in the late 1600s.

Daman lies on Gujarat's southern coast. It has a large tribal population. Farming and fishing are the main occupations. It has the twin cities of **Nani and Moti Daman**, a fort, a lighthouse and Portuguese-style buildings.

The ancient River **Damanganga** lends its name to the region of Daman. It was Damao to the Portuguese. Diu gets its name from the Sanskrit word dvipa or 'island'.

Fact File

Date of formation: May 30, 1987
Size: 112 sq km
Population: 1,58,204
Capital: Daman
Rivers: Damanganga, Kolak, Kalai
Languages: Gujarati, Hindi, Marathi
Neighbours: Gujarat

Dadra & Nagar Haveli are on the

border of Maharashtra and Gujarat. The region is made up largely of hilly forests. River Damanganga and its tributaries Varna, Pipri and Sakartond flow from here to nearby Daman and into the Arabian Sea.

Not much is known about this region's ancient history. The **Koli chieftains** here were defeated by a Rajput prince in 1262. Nagar Haveli remained in Rajput control till the mid-1700s, when the Marathas took over. It was given to the Portuguese in 1783 as a compensation for a warship which the Marathas had destroyed.

Gujarat lies to the north of the region, while Maharashtra lies to its south. Dadra and Nagar Haveli are actually separated from each other by a 3 km portion of Gujarat. Together they have 70 or so villages.

The **ghangal** is a musical instrument made with a gourd, bamboo and iron strings. It is a part of Warli religious rituals. Dances like Tarpha, Gherria, Tur, Thali, the acrobatic Dhol and the masked Bhawada are performed during rituals and festivals.

Carles da Cruz, a Goan teacher and freedom fighter, began a movement to free the region with the encouragement of other Goan nationalists like T B Cunha and the Gujarati kings. The United Front of Goans led by Francis Mascarenhas was supported by tribal groups. Together they drove out Portuguese officers in July 1954. The larger Nagar Haveli was freed a few days later.

Many **tribes** like the Warlis, Kokanas, Bhils, Dhodias, Kathodis, Nayakas, Kolgas and Dublas live here. Most are farmers who grow rice, wheat, sugarcane, catechew or kattha, oilseeds, fruits, pulses and vegetables. They speak languages and dialects like Bhili and Bhilodi.

Fact File

- **Date of formation**: August 11, 1961
- **Size**: 491 sq km
- **Population**: 2,20,490
- **Capital**: Silvassa
- **Rivers**: Silvassa, Khanvel
- **Languages**: Gujarati, Marathi, Hindi, Konkani, Bhili, Bhilodi
- **Neighbours**: Maharashtra, Gujarat

Puducherry or 'the new settlement' in Tamil,

was once known as Pondicherry, and used to be the capital of French India. After 1962, it was merged with other French enclaves like Karaikal and Yanam (on the east coast), and Mahe (on the west coast) to form Puducherry, a Union Territory.

Being on the coast, Puducherry had ancient trade links with the world. **Arikamedu** town nearby traded pottery, beads, precious stones, shell bangles and textiles with Romans in exchange for wine, olive oil and garum or fish sauce in the 1st century AD.

The Pallavas, Cholas, Pandyas and the Vijayanagara Empire ruled Puducherry. From 1638 the **Sultan of Bijapur** took over Gingee. The Portuguese set up a factory here in the early 1500s, but were chased away by the Sultan, only to be replaced by the Danes and the Dutch.

The **French**, who had trading centres in Madras, Mahe and the north, were first invited here to oppose the Dutch. From 1674, Puducherry changed hands between the Dutch, the French and the English. The French ruled here from 1816. Built in the 1700s on a grid pattern, Puducherry has houses built in the Franco-Tamil architectural style.

Karaikal is just 135 km from Puducherry on the east coast. Once ruled by Cholas, the Vijaynagara Empire, Marathas and Muslim rulers, it came under French rule in 1739. Karaikal lies in River Kaveri's fertile delta and grows rice. It has coastal fishing villages and exports fish and shells. The Tsunami of 2004 hit Karaikal badly.

In 1910, **Sri Aurobindo**, freedom fighter and spiritualist, came to French Pondicherry. The Aurobindo Ashram, founded in 1926, was looked after by his French disciple, Mirra Alfassa, also known as The Mother.

Mahe is about 650 km away from Puducherry on the west coast in Kerala. Known as Mayyazhi or the 'sea's eyebrow', the French took it over officially in 1725. It has two parts: Mahe town on the left bank of the River Mayyazhi, and on the right, Naluthara, made up of villages like Chambara, Chalakara, Palour and Pandakkal.

Yanam lies about 850 km away in northeast Andhra Pradesh near the River Godavari. Once part of the Chola Empire, it was fought over by Indian rulers, the British and the French. Finally, in 1731, the French took over. In 1954, Yanam was freed by local nationalists with the help of Dadala Raphael Ramanayya, a freedom fighter.

- **Date of formation:** January 7, 1963
- **Size: Puducherry:** 290 sq km, **Mahe:** 9 sq km, **Yanam:** 20 sq km, **Karaikal:** 161 sq km
- **Population:** 9,74,345
- **Capital:** Puducherry
- **Rivers:** Gingee, Mayyazhi, Gauthami, Arasalar
- **Languages:** Tamil, English, French, Malayalam, Telugu, Hindi
- **Neighbours: Puducherry and Karaikal:** Tamil Nadu, **Mahe:** Kerala, **Yanam:** Andhra Pradesh

Lakshadweep lies to the southwest of India in the Arabian Sea. It is an archipelago or arc of 12 atolls, three reefs and five submerged banks. It is about 300 km from Kerala. Only 10 of its 36 islands are inhabited.

Amini, Kadmat, Kiltan, Chetlat and Bitra islands are together called the **Aminidivi Islands**. The other inhabited islands are Kavaratti, Agatti, Andrott, Kalpeni and Minicoy. The Aminidivis lie to the north; Minicoy or Milaku, the southernmost island, is closer to the Maldives. There are many uninhabited islands, islets and reefs.

Lakshadweep was ruled by **Kerala dynasties** like the Kulasekharas, Chirakkal Rajahs, the Kolathiris and the Arakkals of Kannur in Kerala. The Portuguese came here in the late 1400s, drawn by the islanders' fine coir. In the 1700s, Tipu Sultan took over. When he died in 1799, the British seized Aminidivi and let the Bibi or Queen rule in exchange of an annual tribute.

Bananas, jackfruit, colocasia, wild almonds, different kinds of coconuts and shrubs like kanni grow here. Sea-grasses growing on the beaches prevent erosion. The islands are home to water birds like tharathasi and karifettu or the sooty tern. Crabs and fishes like parrot fish, **butterfly fish** and surgeon fish are abundant.

Most Aminidivi islanders were Mapillahs or Muslims from Kerala. They followed marumakkathayam, the Malayali tradition of descent from the mother's line. The islands were ruled by Bibis or queens. **Kolkali**, Parichakali, Lava, Kattuvili and Oppana are popular folk dances here.

Though the territory is only 32 sq km in size, Lakshadweep's **lagoons** cover an area of 4200 sq km. With its islands, islets, reefs and banks spread out, Lakshadweep has 20,000 sq km of territorial waters. 'Lakshadweep' means 'a hundred thousand islands' in Malayalam. The British used to call it 'Laccadives'.

A lagoon is an area of sea water surrounded by coral reefs or islands. These coral reefs or islands are called atolls. Corals are the hard shells of micro-organisms called polyps, which build the atolls. The English word 'atoll' comes from the Dhivehi **'atholhu'**. It is illegal to pick up any coral found lying around in Lakshadweep.

Malayalam is spoken on most islands. But on Minicoy they speak **Mahl**, a dialect of Dhivehi, the national language of Maldives. Dhivehi is related to Sinhala, and has Malayalam, Hindi, French, English, Arabic and Portuguese words. It is the only Indo-Aryan language found so far south.

Fishing, growing coconuts and making coir (fibre made of coconut husk) are the main activities here. **Coir-making** is a cottage industry, though there are government mills as well. Traditional boats called odams are still built and used. Tuna is processed on Minicoy.

Fact File

- **Date of formation:** November 1, 1956
  Size: 32 sq km
  Population: 60,650
- **Capital:** Kavaratti
  Forests and NPs: Pitti (Bird Island) WS
  Languages: Malayalam, Mahl, Tamil, Hindi
  Neighbours: Kerala, Karnataka
- **State Animal:** Butterfly fish
  State Bird: Sooty tern
  State Tree: Bread fruit

Andaman & Nicobar

islands lie in an arc to the southeast of India. They lie between Myanmar and Sumatra in Indonesia. The islands were a naval base for Kanhoji Angre, the Maratha Admiral, in the 1700s. The British ruled it from the late 1700s. They were interrupted by Japanese rule here from 1942 to 1945. Apart from tribes or indigenous people, the islands are home to many people from the Indian subcontinent.

Port Blair, the Andamans' capital, was first colonised by the British in 1789. The attempt failed and it was re-established as a penal colony in 1858. Freedom fighters and convicts were sent here to be isolated and tortured. They were made to build roads, prisons and harbours.

The **Cellular Jail** was built here between 1896 and 1906. It has three storeys and seven wings that spread outwards from a central tower. There were 698 cells which were designed so that the prisoners would stay isolated from one another.

The 300 or more islands of Andaman are divided into the **Great and the Little Andamans**. The islands of North, Middle and South Andaman make up the Great Andamans. Landfall, Interview, Sentinel, Rutland Islands and Ritchie's Archipelago are some of the other islands. Little Andaman lies to the south. The terrain is mostly hilly, with very little flat land or fresh water. About 30 of the islands are inhabited.

Few of Andaman's tribes survive. The Great Andamanese of Strait Island, Onges of Little Andaman, **Jarawas** of South and Middle Andaman, the Sentinelese of the Sentinel Islands (probably the only surviving **Paleolithic** or Old Stone Age people), and the Shompens of Great Nicobar are some of them. In northern Andaman some tribes of the Yerewa group survive.

Nicobar has a more varied terrain. Among its 22 islands, only about 12—like Car, Camorta, Katchall, Nancowry and Great Nicobar—are occupied. Great Nicobar, which is near Sumatra, is among the few islands which have fresh water.

Andamanese languages can be divided into two sub-groups: the Great Andamanese group and the Ongan group. Onge and Jarawa in the Ongan group have about 100 to 300 speakers. Most Great Andamanese languages are now dead or extinct. Only Aka-Jero is still spoken by a few. Sentinelese has about 50 speakers, but since they have never been in contact with outsiders, their language is unknown.

Great Nicobar island has the large **Great Nicobar Biosphere Reserve**. It has birds and animals like the Nicobar scrubfowl, Malayan box turtle, giant leatherback sea turtle, giant robber crab or the coconut crab and the Nicobar long-tailed macaque or the crab-eating macaque. The Reserve includes the Campbell Bay NP and the Galathea NP.

The **Shompens and the Nicobaris** are the people who lived on Nicobar originally. The Shompens were probably here first. They are isolated, semi-nomadic and live in the Great Nicobar Biosphere Reserve. Nicobaris live on other islands as well. They enjoy music, dance and football. Nicobari languages belong to the Mon-khmer family, while the Shompen language is probably an 'isolate', or a language that shows no links to other language families.

The **dugong** is a vegetarian mammal that lives in the sea and eats sea grasses. It belongs to the Sirenia family. In the olden days, sailors often thought that dugongs and other Sirenias were mermaids. Dugongs are highly endangered by fishing nets, poaching, disappearing sea-grasses, speeding boats and the blasting of coral reefs near their habitats.

An earthquake in the Indian Ocean off Sumatra in December 2004 led to huge **Tsunami** waves. Being closest to Sumatra, Andaman and Nicobar were among the worst hit, with some of the waves reaching a height of 15 m. Thousands of people died or went missing. Entire Nicobari Islands were swept away. Some tribes survived because they lived inland and on higher ground.

Fact File

Date of formation: November 1, 1956
Size: 8249 sq km
Population: 3,56,152
Capital: Port Blair
Rivers: Alexandra, Dagmar, Galathea (Great Nicobar), Kalpong (Andaman)
Forests and NPs: Mahatma Gandhi Marine NP, Middle Button Island NP, Saddle Peak NP, Campbell Bay NP, Galathea Bay NP
Languages: Hindi, Tamil, Bengali, Malayalam, Kannada, Oriya, Nicobarese
Neighbours: None
State Animal: Dugong
State Bird: Andaman wood pigeon
State Tree: Andaman padauk

Are you curious ?

What is a Biosphere Reserve?

The earth's biodiversity—or the variety of life on it—is reducing at an alarming rate. Biosphere Reserves work to maintain a balance between the people who have been living in forests for centuries, and the forest creatures.
They were first created by UNESCO or the United Nations Educational, Scientific and Cultural Organization under the Man and Biosphere program in 1971. There are 531 Biosphere Reserve sites across 105 countries in the world. They are part of a large network and exchange information with each other.

What is Project Tiger?

Tigers are important because they show us how healthy and diverse an ecosystem is. From an estimated 45,000 tigers at the beginning of this century, India probably has less than 1500 tigers today. Tigers are hunted and poached for sport, and for their skin and bones which are used as medicines. With forests being cut, their homes and habitats are also disappearing.
A tiger census in 1972 showed that few tigers remained. Alarmed by this, the Indian government began a program called Project Tiger in 1973. The tiger was declared the national animal to ensure that Tiger Reserves would get special attention and stronger conservation efforts.

What is a Ramsar Site or a Wetland of International Importance?

Wetlands are ecologically important. To think of ways to protect them, a meeting or Convention on Wetlands of International Importance was held in Ramsar, Iran, on February 2, 1971. The Ramsar Convention, as it is called, named about 1838 wetlands in the world as being of international importance. February 2 is celebrated as World Wetlands Day. About 25 Indian wetlands are on the Ramsar list as Wetlands of International Importance. They are known as Ramsar Sites.

What is a National Park?

With so many human beings on earth, more and more forests are being cut down. To preserve the earth's biodiversity, governments the world over have set aside forests which will be kept in a natural state, where animals, birds, trees and land will be left unharmed. These spaces can be of different kinds, called National Parks, Wildlife Sanctuaries or Reserves. Not only do they preserve rare species, they also purify the air we breathe and act as the earth's lungs.

What is a wetland?

Swamps, marshes and bogs make up wetlands—places that are filled with water in some seasons or at all times of the year. The water in a wetland can be moving or it may stand in one place; it can be salty, or fresh or even brackish (a mix of salt and fresh waters). Wetlands are often found between a water body like a sea and the land, and are also known as 'boundary ecosystems'. Wetlands have a lot of biodiversity or variety of life in them, starting with plants like mangroves and water lilies, to reptiles, birds and amphibians. Many delicate and unique wetland ecosystems have been drained to make way for houses or farms.

What is a mangrove forest?

A mangrove is a plant that is specially equipped to grow and thrive in the salty water of a wetland. The roots of mangrove trees are good habitats for small marine creatures like crabs, algae, oysters and sponges. Mangrove roots slow down the flow of water, thus preventing erosion and floods. The Sundarbans Mangrove Forest, at the mouth of the Ganga and between India and Bangladesh, is one of the largest in the world. It is a World Heritage Site.

What is a primate? How is an ape different from a monkey?

Primates are mammals with five-fingered hands, a poor sense of smell, nails instead of claws on their feet and a large brain. Monkeys, apes and humans are primates. Unlike a monkey, an ape does not have a tail. It has a more complex brain and an appendix. Chimpanzees, bonobos, orangutans, humans and gorillas are apes. Gibbons are the apes found in Southeast Asia. They have longer arms, thicker fur and can make loud hooting calls which are heard over great distances. The hoolock gibbon is the only ape found in India.

What is a World Heritage site?

Some monuments and forests are so beautiful and valuable that they belong to not just the country where they are, but to all the people of the world. They are a part of humanity's common heritage. The word 'heritage' means a gift from the past. UNESCO has identified many sites in the world that are a part of our shared heritage. The Ancient City of Sigiriya in Sri Lanka, the Imperial Palaces of China, the wilds of Serengeti in Kenya, Egyptian pyramids, and 27 places in India are on this prestigious list.

What do Paleolithic, Mesolithic and Neolithic mean?

Prehistoric human culture is divided into Stone Age, Bronze Age and Iron Age, depending on the kinds of tools that human beings were using during the time. The Stone Age is the first period. During this time, humans used tools made of stones to cut and carve things.

The Paleolithic or the Old Stone Age is the first period of the Stone Age. At this time, very basic stone tools were used.

During the Mesolithic or Middle Stone Age, more advanced stone tools called microliths were made.

The Neolithic or New Stone Age was the last part of the Stone Age. Stone tools were made by grinding or polishing them. It was around this time that people began weaving, making pottery, living in villages and keeping domestic animals.

 What are megaliths, monoliths, menhirs and dolmens?

Megaliths are large stones which stand in a group. They were used for social or religious reasons. They were sometimes places where people buried their dead. Monoliths are large stones which usually stand alone. A statue or a sculpture carved out of a single piece of rock is also called a monolithic statue. The statue of Gomateshwara is the tallest freestanding monolithic statue in the world.

Menhirs are single, upright prehistoric monoliths. Dolmens have a horizontal stone slab supported by two or more vertical stones—like a table.

 What is a Stupa?

A Stupa is a dome-shaped structure where relics of the Buddha were buried. The rounded shape was probably inspired by the pre-Buddhist burial mounds. Ancient Stupas in India were found in places like Dhamek, Sanchi and Sopara near Mumbai.

 What is a chaitya?

A chaitya is a large prayer hall made of rock and teak wood, with an apse or a half-dome-shaped gap at one end. Karla and Bhaja caves, in Maharashtra, have large and elaborate chaityas.

What is a vihara?

'Vihara' is a Sanskrit and Pali word that means a shelter. Originally, a vihara was a place where wandering Buddhist monks would take shelter during the rainy season. They were located on trade routes. Most of them were rock-cut and had cells for monks to sleep in, with beds and pillows cut out of rocks. Slowly, viharas became places of worship, meditation and learning—like the Mahaviharas at Nalanda and Nagarjunakonda.

 What is a Union Territory?

A Union Territory is an administrative division of India which does not have its own elected government, but is ruled directly by the central government. Delhi and Puducherry have been given partial statehood with legislative assemblies and councils of ministers that have limited power.

My Amazing India

Have you travelled to any part of India?
Make your own Amazing India pages
by sticking a few pictures
of the place and writing about it.
Use the blank spaces here
or make your own scrapbook.

I went to ....
The weather there was..
I ate special food called...
I saw monuments like...
There are crafts like...
The place is famous for..
I enjoyed..
....
....
....
But I did not like...
....
....
Some memories I have of my visit are...
....
....
....
....
....
....

Draw or stick pictures here

Stick photo here

I also saw

I also saw

Stick photo here

Stick photo here

I also saw